Gulf Coast Secrets

Blackbird Beach, book two

Maggie Miller

Maggie Miller

GULF COAST SECRETS: Blackbird Beach, book 2
Copyright © 2021 Maggie Miller

All rights reserved. No part of this book may be reproduced in any form or by any electronic or mechanical means, including information storage and retrieval systems—except in the case of brief quotations embodied in critical articles or reviews—without permission in writing from the author.

This book is a work of fiction. The characters, events, and places portrayed in this book are products of the author's imagination and are either fictitious or are used fictitiously. Any similarity to real person, living or dead, is purely coincidental and not intended by the author.

Sign up for Maggie's mailing list via her website, www.MaggieMillerAuthor.com, to find out when her next book comes out!

Gulf Coast Secrets

Escape to the Gulf Coast of Florida with Georgia Carpenter as she gets a second chance at life, love, and happiness.

With the full realization of her inheritance before her, Georgia Carpenter is overwhelmed by the generosity of her late great aunt. What lays ahead of Georgia, however, is more work than she's ever done in her life.

Then another family member arrives unexpectedly, and things change in a way she never imagined possible. But what's another curveball in the crazy game of life?

She thinks she can handle everything being thrown at her, along with the help of Travis Taylor, the handsome handyman she inherited from aunt. That is until her cheating husband does something that could destroy her chance to start over.

Maggie Miller

Gulf Coast Secrets

Chapter One

Georgia couldn't believe her eyes as she stared at her rain-soaked son, Griffin, and the infant in his arms, standing on the front porch of the cottage. "Griff, honey, come in. What are you doing here? It's so good to see you. Is everything all right? What's going on?"

"A lot. Obviously." He stepped inside, shedding drops of water everywhere. "I should have called, but I didn't want to tell you all of this over the phone."

"All of what?" Her head was spinning. Why was there a baby in his arms?

Mia, her daughter, came into the kitchen from the living room. "Is that Griff I hear? Oh, wow. Hey, Griff, it *is* you. And you have a baby. That's new." She blinked like she wasn't sure she was really seeing what she was seeing.

"Yeah," he said. "She sure is. This is Chloe. My daughter."

Georgia took a long, deep breath as she tried to process that information. "I didn't even know you were seeing anyone." Then her heart tightened in her chest as his words registered. "I have a granddaughter."

Griffin nodded, smiling. "You want to hold her?"

"More than anything in the world." Georgia felt like her entire body was filled with stars, each one a pinpoint of love that hadn't existed a moment ago. Explanations could wait.

He handed the sleeping child to her and Georgia cradled her close, marveling at her tiny, perfect fingers clutching the blanket. And the tiny perfect fingernails at the ends of those fingers. Everything about her was perfect. "Hi Chloe."

Overwhelmed with love, she looked up at her son. "She's amazing."

"She is." He nodded and for the first time, she saw how tired and worn down he looked.

Unable to resist, Georgia bent, kissed her granddaughter's downy head, and inhaled. There was nothing better than the smell of a baby. Especially one who was your first grandchild.

"So many questions, Griff." Mia shook her head. "But it's so good to see you."

"You too, kiddo." He held his arms out.

Mia stepped toward him and hugged him hard before moving back to look at him closely. "You look beat. Why don't you come into the living room and tell us the whole thing?"

"Yes," Georgia said. "Come in, sit down and—"

"I should get her bag out of the car." Griff hooked his thumb over his shoulder. "She'll need a bottle soon. And a diaper."

Georgia hesitated, a sudden flash of a scenario playing through her head where Griffin dropped off the baby and disappeared. But he wouldn't do that, would he? "You want an umbrella?"

"Nah, I'm already wet."

"Okay, grab her stuff. Then let's talk."

"We will." He blew out a breath. "Be right back."

"So will I," Mia said. She went into her room.

Georgia watched out the window while he jogged to his Jeep in the rain, retrieved the bag and jogged back. She'd held her breath until he'd made the turn back toward the house. But Griffin wasn't that kind of guy. She should have known better. She was just a little overwhelmed.

He came in, soaked again, and put the baby bag on the kitchen table.

Mia had already returned with a towel. "Here." She tossed it to him.

He caught it and wiped his face. "Thanks." He dried his hair a little too. "Could I use your bathroom? Long drive."

"Absolutely," Georgia said. "Do you want something to eat or drink?"

He nodded. "That would be great. Thanks, Mom."

Mia tipped her head. "Come on, you can use my bathroom."

As they left, Georgia stared down at the bundle in her arms again. Chloe. Her granddaughter. A marvel of tiny pink perfection.

Georgia had never loved anyone so much or so fast in her life. She inhaled the baby's sweet, powdery fragrance once again. "You precious thing."

One-handed, she got a container of the last of the leftover spaghetti out of the fridge and into the microwave and set the timer.

Mia came in. "Go on, I'll take care of fixing him a plate."

"Thanks." Georgia carried the infant into the living room and sat in the chair. Clyde, the big orange cat she'd inherited from her late great Aunt Norma, along with the two cottages and the Sea Glass Inn between them, paid no attention to the new person in the room.

Georgia had a feeling that would change if Chloe started to cry. Although she seemed pretty contentedly asleep at the moment.

Griffin came out from Mia's bedroom. He noticed Clyde right away. "I didn't know you had a cat."

Mia answered as she joined them. "Clyde was Aunt Norma's cat so now he's ours. He's good company. And a very good boy. Aren't you, Clyde?"

Clyde looked up at her and made a few biscuits on the towel he was laying on. Mia had put it on the couch where he liked to lay in an effort to keep the hair contained. It was only marginally working.

"How about I tell you all about Chloe," Griffin said. "And then you tell me all about Aunt Norma?"

"Deal," Georgia said.

The microwave timer dinged.

"I put some leftover spaghetti in to heat up for you," Georgia said.

Mia headed for the kitchen. "I'll get it. You sit, Griff."

"Thanks." He took a seat on the couch, gave Clyde a little scratch on the head, and sighed. "So…"

Gulf Coast Secrets

Mia came back with a plate of spaghetti and a glass of water. "Here you go. Unless you want some wine?"

"No, I'm good." He took the food and drink from her. "Thanks."

He set the glass on the coffee table, then immediately picked up the fork and dug in. He took a big bite, chewed a little, then began. "I was dating this girl, Olivia, for a while. She was a little…high strung but beautiful. I met her on one of the shoots. Swimsuit model."

Georgia couldn't stop her brows from lifting in response.

He held up the hand with the fork in it. "I know, don't even start. Like I said, she was beautiful, and she said yes when I asked her out, and I'm a guy, so we dated. But after a couple months, she made it pretty clear why she was dating me. She wanted someone who could help her get better jobs. Book bigger gigs. Maybe get her in a magazine. Basically someone more powerful than me."

Mia rolled her eyes. "Nice girl."

He shrugged. "I kind of expected it, honestly. And after a couple months, I forgot about her. It's not like we were in love or anything."

Georgia listened intently, her gut telling her exactly where this was going.

"Then," he continued around another mouthful of spaghetti, "about two weeks ago, I get a knock on my door. I go to see who it is and no one's there. Except for a baby carrier with Chloe in it. Her baby bag was there, and she had a note tucked in beside her."

"Are you serious?" Mia said. "Who does that?"

Griffin shook his head. "As best I can tell, Olivia."

Maggie Miller

"As best you can tell?" Georgia asked. "You mean you don't know for sure?"

"No. There was no birth certificate, and the note wasn't signed. It just said this is your child. You'd better take care of her. And that was it." He sighed. "What else was I supposed to do?"

"Um, paternity test maybe?" Mia asked.

He nodded. "I did that immediately. Chloe's definitely mine. But I don't know her birthday or how old she is."

Georgia held the bundle in her arms a little closer. What a sad start for such a precious child. "I'd say she's about three or four months old. I bet a pediatrician could give you a more accurate assessment. You need to take her anyway. She'll need her shots, if she hasn't had them."

"Yeah, that's about what I figured out for her age, too, based on when Olivia and I were seeing each other. But I should take her to a doctor. And not just for the shots. I don't know when her last checkup was. I've been so focused on getting through each day that I didn't think about that too much." Griffin blew out another breath. "It's kind of crazy how hard it is to take care of a baby. I had to bring her along on a shoot with me because I had no one to watch her, but she was such a distraction that I got fired."

Mia frowned. "Whoever did that to you was a heartless jerk."

"Oh, honey," Georgia said. "I'm so sorry." She made a mental note to call Roger Gillum in the morning. Not only did she need to see where he was on her soon-to-be ex's claim on her inheritance, but now she wanted to ask him a few things about her son's situation.

Gulf Coast Secrets

"Thanks. Anyway, I'm sorry to just show up like this but it seemed easier than trying to explain everything and the bottom line is I need help. I'm a little out of my depth here."

Mia laughed softly. "Plus you knew that if you showed up and put that baby in Mom's arms, there was no way she'd turn you down."

One corner of his mouth quirked up. "Maybe a little of that too."

Georgia shook her head, her previous thoughts returning. "You're not trying to drop her off and leave, are you?"

Griffin frowned and his retort was sharp. "No. Chloe is my daughter. My responsibility. I'd never leave her. Having that happen to her once in her life is one time too many already."

"Good," Georgia said. Her heart swelled at her son's sudden and fierce protection of his child.

"But I was hoping I could get some help. Especially if I move here."

"Get out," Mia said. She was smiling, clearly pleased by the news. "You're going to move here?"

"Chloe changes everything. She needs to grow up around family. And I need help with her. I don't think I can do it alone. Besides, I can be a photographer anywhere." He shrugged. "So why not do it where my family is?"

"Of course, we'll help," Georgia said. She was as pleased as Mia, maybe more so, but couldn't stop thinking about how tough a road her son had in front of him. Moving wasn't going to help that. "Do you think you'll be able to find work right away?"

"I hope so." He finished the last bite of spaghetti, then drank about half the glass of water. "I'll do whatever I have to. Mop floors, haul trash, flip burgers, I don't care. Work is work. And I'll just keep the photography as a side hustle until it becomes enough to support us full time."

Georgia nodded, proud of Griffin for understanding what it was going to take. "Sounds like you know what you have to do."

He smiled tentatively. "There's just one other thing. I was hoping I could stay with you guys. Just until I get on my feet. Which I promise to work hard to make happen."

Mia looked at her mom and shrugged. "I do have that extra bed in my room. It's just a twin, but whatever."

"Of course," Georgia said. She wasn't about to turn her son and granddaughter out. The cottage was small, but they were all family. "What about Chloe? We don't have a crib."

Griffin glanced at his daughter. "I have a Pack-n-Play. And her car seat can also be disconnected and used as a carrier. I guess she'll have to sleep in the Pack-n-Play until I get a proper crib."

"You know," Mia said to Georgia. "I think there's a crib in the attic at the Inn." She looked at her brother again. "We're moving over there soon and then we're going to rent this place out so Mom can start earning some money."

"Oh." Griffin's face fell. "I guess I'll need to work pretty fast then."

Georgia shook her head. She wasn't about to allow her son and grandchild to be homeless. "We'll figure something out."

He nodded but looked unconvinced. "So tell me about the inn. How did it all come about?"

Gulf Coast Secrets

"Well," Georgia said. "Let me tell you." She launched into the story from the very beginning when she got the call from Aunt Norma's attorney, Roger Gillum, at the moment when she was moving out of the studio apartment she could no longer afford. From there, she told Griffin how Mia had called her right afterwards to say that she'd found out about Brendan cheating on her and needed a place to stay.

Griffin looked at Mia. "Are you serious? That jerk."

Mia nodded. "Yep. But it's water under the bridge. I mean, I still hate him and Sarah, my ex-friend that he was sleeping with, but he can have her. I already mailed his engagement ring back to him."

"Good for you. That idiot doesn't deserve you."

"He really doesn't," Mia said.

Griffin looked at his mother again. "So what then? You both came over here to the cottage?"

Georgia shifted Chloe in her arms. "Yes. I didn't realize at the time that not only had I inherited this cottage but also another cottage, and the inn that sits between them. I was in such a hurry to get over here, that I cut Mr. Gillum off before he could tell me the entire story."

Mia laughed softly. "Yeah, it was kind of a shocker when she found out just how much she had inherited. But the inn needs some work. We've been spending all of our time over there fixing the place back up. Thankfully, Aunt Norma left mom some money to take care of those things that need doing."

Griffin's brows shot up. "That's really good."

"Even better?" Mia made a coy face. "She also left Mom her hot handyman. Travis."

Maggie Miller

Georgia rolled her eyes. "Your sister seems to think that Mr. Taylor and I are more than friends. We are not. But we are very lucky to have him helping us. He lives in the second cottage. It's part of his employment package."

"Whatever," Mia said. "Mom's totally into him. Which is cool, because he's a very nice guy. He already taught me how to change the flapper valve in a toilet."

Griffin looked skeptical. "You know how to change a toilet valve?"

"Yep. I did almost all of them at the inn myself."

"And the toilets still work?"

She stuck her tongue out at him. "Yes, goofball, they do."

"Wow." He laughed. "I'm impressed."

Chloe let out a gasp, then a whimper.

Griffin got up. "She's hungry. I'll go fix her bottle. After she has that, I'll get my camera equipment out of the Jeep. I don't want to leave all of that out there. I can get the rest in the morning when hopefully the rain has stopped."

"This is a pretty safe area," Georgia said. "But no point in tempting anyone."

Chloe whimpered again.

"I'm getting it, baby girl." He went off to the kitchen.

Georgia held Chloe up and made silly faces at her. The child's grumbles were growing louder. One definite sob escaped.

Clyde jumped off the couch and slunk away to Mia's room.

"What's a matter, baby?" Georgia said to her granddaughter. "Are you hungry? Your daddy went to get your supper, sweetheart. Just a minute now. Who's the prettiest baby there is? Who's the prettiest baby?"

Gulf Coast Secrets

Georgia put Chloe over her shoulder and patted her gently on the back. Whatever they had to do to work things out so that Griffin and Chloe had a place to stay, they'd do.

Family came first.

Maggie Miller

Gulf Coast Secrets

Chapter Two

Mia bounced Chloe on her shoulder. Being an aunt was incredibly cool. For the first time in her life, Mia felt a kind of love and responsibility unlike anything else. She already knew without question that she would die for this child. And that was after knowing her for less than twenty-four hours.

It didn't hurt that Chloe seemed to be a pretty happy baby, too, at least after she'd had a diaper change and her bottle. And despite how tricky making coffee one-handed had been, Mia wasn't about to put her down.

Mia had been glad to take care of Chloe so Griff could get ready for the day. She was also happy today was one of her days off from Ludlow's grocery store. She only worked a few shifts a week and would have loved to work more to bring in extra money, but that's all they'd had an opening for. Still, it was better than nothing.

And it also meant that today she could continue to watch Chloe while her brother went out to look for work. Of course,

She was supposed to be helping paint the kitchen at the inn. She hoped both things would be possible. Especially if she could find the crib she'd thought she had seen in the attic and set that up for Chloe.

Mia's plan was to put the crib and Chloe in the sunny breakfast room next to the kitchen. That way she wouldn't be far from where they were painting in the kitchen, and Mia and Georgia could keep an eye on her, taking care of her whenever she needed them.

Mia hoped Griffin would be able to find some kind of work, but she also knew that coming by a job wasn't going to be the easiest thing. She'd kind of lucked into the one she had but finding any kind of photography work in a town this small wasn't going to be easy. But then again there had to be some sort of work out there, right?

"How do I look?" Griffin asked. He was in dress pants, a button-down shirt, and a slim tie. His hair, which might have been a touch long, had been combed back neatly.

Mia nodded. "You look nice. Very professional. I'd hire you."

"Thanks, but you're a little biased." He laughed as he went to pour himself a cup of coffee. "About that, any ideas on who might be hiring in town?"

"Not a clue, sorry. The grocery store that hired me could only give me a few shifts a week." It had also been the first and only place she'd applied, but she kept that to herself. She didn't want him to think it was going to be that easy just in case it wasn't.

"Okay."

Gulf Coast Secrets

Their mom walked in, dressed for another day of painting at the inn in her paint-splattered jeans and sweatshirt. "You look great. Off to job hunt?"

"Yes, thanks." He nodded, leaning back against the counter with his coffee. "And I'm weirdly nervous about it."

"You'll find something." Georgia got a mug down from the cabinet. "Might not be today, but something will come along. Otherwise, we can always use help getting the inn ready."

"Hey," Mia said, an idea coming to her. "You have all your camera equipment. Once the inn is done, we could use some good shots for the website and Facebook page."

"Sure, no problem. I can do that." He turned slightly, looking toward the beach. "I wonder if I could set up a little wedding photo business. People must get married around here, right? It is a good spot for it."

Georgia smiled. "We're hoping to do weddings at the inn. Small ones, anyway."

"Yeah?" He seemed excited about that. "Hey, that would be all right. I could do the pictures for a great price. It would definitely help me build my portfolio."

Mia sat up a little more, keeping Chloe snug against her. "You know, you could offer all kinds of photos. People are always getting family portraits taken on the beach too. And this beach is beautiful. Really ideal."

He nodded, clearly thinking that over. "I'd love to do that. It would be a great chance to hone my abilities." He drank some of his coffee, still staring toward the beach. "That water does look nice. I wish I had my paddleboard. I bet that's pretty popular around here."

"Beats me," Mia said. "I haven't seen anyone out there on one."

"Really?" He made a face. "That surprises me."

"Where is your paddleboard?"

"Sold it." He drank the rest of his coffee, almost gulping it down. "All right, I'm going to head out. You're sure you're okay watching her?"

"Absolutely. We'll be at the inn if you need us." Mia grinned at Chloe. "We're going to have a lovely day, aren't we, Chloe girl?"

Clyde hopped up onto the chair beside Mia, his whiskers quivering with interest as he peered at the baby.

Chloe reached out for him, her little fingers wiggling, and managed to grab hold of one of his ears.

Everyone seemed to hold their breath for a moment, then Clyde leaned into her little hand with his eyes half shut.

Mia smiled. "I think he likes her."

Griffin leaned in and kissed Chloe's cheek. "Be nice to the kitty, sweetheart." Then he looked at Mia. "And you make sure the kitty's nice to her. I don't want to come home and find scratches on my child."

"Settle down. Clyde's a gentle giant. Now, go find a job."

He grabbed his keys off the table where he'd left them. "I plan on it." He kissed Georgia on the cheek, too. "Thanks, Mom. For letting us stay."

She smiled. "Thanks for bringing me a grandbaby."

He grinned right back. "You're welcome. See you later. Bye Chloe. Daddy loves you." And with that, he was out the door.

Gulf Coast Secrets

As he drove away, Mia looked at her mother. "Can you believe Griff is a father?"

"And he seems to be doing a decent job of it too." Georgia took a deep breath. "We're going to have to figure out the living situation, though."

"What if I gave them my room at the inn? To share, I mean." Mia knew it would be a sacrifice, but she also knew it wouldn't be forever.

"Kiddo, that is very sweet of you, but you don't know what you're proposing. Sharing a room temporarily with your brother is one thing. Sharing it with him and a baby permanently is something else entirely. Babies wake up a lot. Which means Griffin will be up and down with her, and it also means you won't sleep either. And I need you sharp. I'm kind of counting on you to be the brains of this operation."

Mia sighed. "Yeah. I guess we'll have to see how today goes on the job front for him. But look, I could handle it for a couple weeks. Or we could let him stay here in the cottage."

Georgia nodded. "I thought about that. I really did. And we could probably swing it for a month. But if the inn isn't open and making money soon, we're going to be in a hard spot. Travis's paycheck comes out of that account Aunt Norma left me, too. And while he's not as expensive as some because his job includes his cottage, he's not free either."

"I forgot about that." Mia rubbed Chloe's back while she continued to engage with Clyde, who seemed perfectly happy to be the center of the baby's attention.

"Plus there's insurance that comes out of there too. Electric, water, trash services—"

"I get it. We need to rent this place."

"We do." Georgia put her empty mug in the sink. "But no one's going homeless. We'll figure it out. Right now, I need to get over there and get to work. Travis is going to wonder what happened to us. Don't forget, he's got to finish fixing that shower upstairs and we're supposed to be cutting in the kitchen for painting while he does that. I don't know how long all that tile work is going to take him, but I don't want him to think we're slacking, either."

"Right, I know. I'll be over just as soon as I make sure I have everything I need for her." Mia flipped open the top of the baby bag.

Georgia started ticking things off. "Bottles, diapers, wipes, change of clothes—"

Mia nodded as she found those things in the bag. "I have all that. Plus some other things. Like a stuffed giraffe and a chewable octopus. Diaper rash cream, too." She looked up at her mom. "I think we're good to go. I'll walk with you."

"You'd better bring the car seat in case you can't find the crib you thought you saw."

Mia made a face. "What am I going to do if it's not there? I mean, that could have been a slatted headboard."

"Didn't Griff say he had a Pack-n-Play?"

"Yeah, but that's still in his car which he just drove away in."

"If you can't find the crib, you'll have to call him to bring it back. That child can't stay in a car seat all day."

"No, she can't. She already slept in it last night. I'm sure she's sick of it. All right. That'll be the plan, that I'll call him if there's no crib." She got up, taking Chloe away from Clyde.

Gulf Coast Secrets

Chloe's little face scrunched up and Mia immediately sensed trouble. She sat back down. Chloe reached for Clyde again and smiled.

Mia slanted her eyes at her mom. "I think Clyde needs to come with us."

"He can't. We don't have a litter box set up for him over there and with all that painting going on...I don't think it's a good idea. Let me see what I can do." Georgia held out her hands. "Chloe, baby, come to Mimi."

Chloe looked over at Georgia, her little head wobbling.

Georgia clapped her hands and cooed at her. "Who's the prettiest baby?"

Chloe laughed, distracted.

Maintaining the same goofy expression and babytalk voice, Georgia said, "Let's go now before she looks at Clyde again."

Mia got up, grabbed the baby bag, and headed for the door. She got it open and used her body to block Chloe's sight line of Clyde. Georgia kept her entertained as she left the cottage.

Mia got the door shut and locked, and off they went down the sidewalk. Thankfully, it wasn't raining today like it had been yesterday. Otherwise they would have definitely needed an umbrella as well to protect Chloe from the rain.

The door to the inn was unlocked, a sure sign that Travis was already there. They went in and could hear the sounds of work coming from the upstairs.

"Good morning, Travis," Georgia yelled upstairs. "We're here."

A moment passed before Travis appeared at the top of the steps. "Good morning, ladies." He squinted at them. "I'm pretty sure I would have remembered you having a baby, Mia. Or at least remembered you mentioning it."

"Long story short," Georgia said. "My son showed up last night. This is my granddaughter, Chloe. He's job hunting. So we're babysitting."

Mia nodded. "And I thought I saw a crib in the attic so I'm going to look as soon as I put her in the breakfast room."

"There should be one in there. We had one just in case a guest needed it. If you need help with it let me know. Same thing if you want any help getting set up for the painting. I've already taped some things up and I've got the paint in there. Ladders are up too."

Georgia nodded. "Okay, thanks. I'll yell up if we need something."

They went through the inn, back to the kitchen. Travis had done a lot. The room looked ready to paint. Or would be, after the careful cutting in of all the walls, corners, and around all the door frames and cabinets.

Mia looked at her mom. "I'll be quick. I'm going to put her in the breakfast room, then hustle upstairs to see what I can find."

"Leave her in here with me. I still have to get myself organized and open up the bucket of paint. If I start before you get back, I'll take her in there. Might open a window for her, too. It's nice out. A little fresh air wouldn't hurt."

"Okay." Mia set Chloe's car seat down and put the diaper bag beside it. "Back as soon as I can, kiddo."

She practically jogged up the flights of stairs to the third floor where the attic access was. Thankfully, they'd left that door unlocked because she hadn't thought to bring the key. She opened it, turned on the light, and had a look around.

"Ah hah." There was a crib. At least she thought that's what it was. She went over to have a closer look. Yep, definitely a crib. But she was going to need a mattress for it, too.

She looked around. The attic was a pretty big space and filled with all kinds of things from furniture to stacks of boxes. Behind a dress form in one corner were some things covered in sheets. They were the right size for a crib mattress.

There was no point in hauling the crib out until she knew for sure. She pulled the corner of one sheet back. And found exactly what she was looking for. "Yes."

Now she just had to get it all out and back downstairs. She'd need Travis most likely.

But before she yelled for him she might as well get it all out. She dug out the crib first. It took moving several boxes and a trunk that she would have loved to open, but this wasn't the time. The crib pieces were all zip tied together and there was a baggie of parts attached. Small screws and an allen wrench. "Please let this be easy."

She hauled it to the door just as Travis showed up. "Hey, I was just going to call for you."

He nodded. "I figured you'd need a hand with that."

"Well, you're right. And your timing couldn't be better."

Maggie Miller

Chapter Three

Georgia was ready to open the paint, so she picked Chloe up in her car seat and carried her into the breakfast room, facing her toward the outside. The space was lovely and bright with white walls and pale blue gingham valances over its numerous windows. Two sets of French doors led out to the magnificent deck.

The room held a few tables for two, a couple more that could seat four, and a single large round one that could probably handle six in the center. She put Chloe's car seat on that table, then went over and flipped on the lights even though the space was flooded with sun.

The simple crystal chandeliers flared to life, sparkling and catching's Chloe's gaze. She waved her little hands at them. So cute, Georgia could barely stand it.

Was Chloe the most perfect baby in the world? Or was that just Georgia seeing her through grandma-colored glasses? Georgia smiled. Both. But she was perfect.

Maggie Miller

"Be right back, sweetheart." Georgia retrieved the diaper bag and set it on the long server that sat against the wall dividing the breakfast room from the kitchen. The server was the same color as the blue gingham valances. Georgia had decided that's where the breakfast buffet was usually set up.

She went back to Chloe. "You like those lights? How they sparkle? You might take after your Aunt Norma. Oh, she would have eaten you up." The chandeliers weren't exactly beachy, but they gave the room a slightly French country feeling, which Georgia liked. She didn't want to change a thing in here. Especially not after getting Chloe's coo of approval.

Besides, Aunt Norma's tastes might have been a little eclectic, but that only gave the inn more character.

She heard footsteps, turned, and saw Travis and Mia coming toward her carrying what looked like a crib in parts and a mattress. "You guys need help?"

"No," Travis said. "We got it." He put the crib parts down. They were a beautiful dark wood carved with little vines. Very pretty. "Where do you want this?"

Georgia pointed to the space in front of the server. "I guess right here is fine."

Travis bent and wiggled his fingers at Chloe. "Hiya, princess."

Chloe smiled at him.

He smiled back. "Aren't you a little charmer?"

Mia leaned the mattress against the wall. "There were no sheets with this, so I'll have to find a regular one and wrap it around."

Gulf Coast Secrets

Travis straightened. "Check the linen closet in the laundry room. We didn't use this crib much, but we did use it occasionally. I'm pretty sure there's a set of sheets around somewhere. They ought to be in decent shape, too."

"I'll look in there," Mia said. "If the inn used the crib, does that mean you know how to put this thing together?"

"Yep. I'm the one who took it apart and stored it like this. Give me fifteen minutes. Maybe less."

"Excellent." Mia pointed to the laundry room. "I'll go look for the sheets."

As she went that way, Georgia took a few steps toward the kitchen. "Do you want help? If not, I'm going to start cutting in."

"I could use a little help. Just until I get the rails attached. It's easier if someone's holding the pieces and keeping them upright."

"Sure. What do you want me to hold? The headboard?"

"That's fine, I can start there." He whipped out a pocketknife and cut the zip ties, carefully setting the baggie of screws to the side. Then he laid all the pieces out and held up one large slatted one so that it stood upright. "Here you go. Keep it just like that."

She took hold of it while he opened the baggie, took out a few screws and an allen wrench, and started attaching the first rail.

"So," Travis said. "What's the rest of that long story?"

Georgia took a breath. "Griffin showed up last night about half an hour after we got home. Chloe is almost as new to him as she is to us. She was left on his doorstep with a short note and a diaper bag and not much else."

Maggie Miller

Travis let out a low whistle. "No kidding?"

"No kidding. Taking care of her got him fired from his last job, which was part of why he went quiet on us. Taking care of her and figuring out what to do next."

"Babies are a lot of work. Any idea what happened to her mother?"

"Not really. The note wasn't even signed. In fact, he's only reasonably sure who her mother is based on the timeline of things, but he did get a paternity test done and Chloe is definitely his."

"Good for him then."

Georgia smiled. "Good for me, too."

Travis looked up, grinning. "You do seem to have an extra little glow about you today, grandma."

"Mimi," Georgia said. "I've decided that's what I want to be called."

"Mimi it is then. She's a beautiful child. You said Griffin is job hunting. Does that mean he's here to stay?"

She nodded. "He wants Chloe to grow up around family. And quite frankly, he needs the help."

"I can understand that. What's he do?"

"Photographer by trade. Trying to get his own business up and running."

"He might want to check in with the Blackbird Gazette."

"Oh?"

Travis finished with the first rail and started on the second. "Kelly Singh, she's the editor, she's looking for a photographer. Or was. Not sure if that spot is still open. Her dad, Navi, is my dentist. He mentioned it last week when I was in for a cleaning. Again, that was last week so she might

Gulf Coast Secrets

have filled that spot. Then again, this is Blackbird Beach. Not sure there are that many photographers around here."

With one hand still on the headboard, Georgia took her phone from her back pocket and started texting Griffin.

Travis laughed. "You can let go and use both hands. And hey, it's not a full-time job so don't get too excited about it. Pretty sure it's on an as-needed basis. Like when there's a high school game or a council meeting. That sort of thing."

"Even so," Georgia said as she tapped the screen. "It's something and it's in his field." *Try the Blackbird Gazette. Local paper. Looking for photographer.* She hit send, then looked at Travis. "Thank you for that."

"No problem, Mimi."

Thank you, will do! Griffin texted back.

She laughed more at Travis than Griffin's quick response, shaking her head as she tucked her phone back in her pocket. The name Mimi was going to make her smile for a long time to come. "How's it going with that bathroom upstairs?"

"Dried up pretty good overnight, so I got the new greenboard in to replace the water-damaged section of drywall. After this, I'll mix up some grout and get the tile put back on. While that sets up, I'll be able to help you paint." He didn't look up from the section he was attaching. "We may not get the kitchen done today."

She shrugged. "Not much can be done about that."

"Nope. Especially not with the HVAC contractor coming out here this afternoon to run a check on the system. The good news is the paint should be dry enough in the bedrooms by the morning so you and Mia could move into tomorrow. If you're ready."

Maggie Miller

"Both are good news, really. So long as the system doesn't need anything major and cost a fortune."

"Probably just a freon charge." He glanced at her. "Are you going to move over here then?"

"Definitely."

"Not that it's any of my business, but where are you going to put Griffin?"

"With me." Mia walked back in, a set of white sheets patterned with yellow rubber ducks in her arms. "Found the sheets. I'm going to wash them real quick. We can just put her blanket down for now."

Travis looked at her with obvious uncertainty. "You're going to share that second bedroom with your brother and a baby?"

"I know, I know," she said. "Babies cry and don't sleep, so I won't either. But we don't have much choice. We need to get the other cottage rented and get some money coming in. And it'll only be temporary."

She hugged the sheets to her chest. "Griff will find a job and then he'll be able to get a place of his own."

"That might not happen for a while. Even if the Gazette is still hiring, I don't think it's going to be the kind of money that'll get him his own place. Not for a while, anyway," Travis said.

Mia shrugged. "Maybe he'll get two jobs. I could always ask at Ludlow's if they need some help stocking. There's got to be something out there."

Travis started on the last section of crib. "Georgia, I realize you have skin in this game, but what kind of a man is your son?"

Gulf Coast Secrets

Odd question, she thought, but then again, maybe Travis had thought of another job opportunity. "A lot like Mia. Hard worker. Smart. Ambitious."

Travis nodded slowly. "He can have the second bedroom in my cottage."

Maggie Miller

Chapter Four

Griffin wanted this job so bad he could taste it. If the last two weeks had taught him anything it was how expensive diapers and formula were.

Add on rent for an apartment, car insurance, groceries, utilities—he took a breath. He *needed* this job.

With his portfolio under his arm, he straightened his tie, lifted his chin, then strode into the office of the Blackbird Gazette with a smile on his face. He did his best to exude more confidence than he felt.

There were a couple desks, but only the center one was occupied by a pretty, dark-haired woman who was intently peering at her computer.

"Good morning."

She looked up at him over the rims of her glasses. Her hair was a messy bun with a pencil stuck through it. "Good morning. How can I help you?"

"I was told the paper is looking for a photographer?"

"Yes, that's right." She stood up and pushed her glasses on top of her head. Only the messy bun seemed to stop them from sliding all the way back. "But I haven't even put a second notice up."

"A second notice?"

"We hired a photographer last week, but they got a better offer in Tampa, so it fell through. I was about to relist the notice today. How did you know?"

"My mom told me. I'm not sure how she knew. My mom owns the inn. Well, she just inherited it. She's working on getting it back in shape so she can open it again." He was rambling. He tended to do that when he was nervous. Which he was, because not only did he really want this job but the woman behind the desk was remarkably beautiful.

"The Sea Glass Inn?" she asked.

He wasn't sure if that's what it was called but that was the name of the street, so he nodded. "It used to be owned by my Aunt Norma Merriweather."

The woman smiled a little sadly. "Norma was such a fixture in Blackbird Beach. I can't speak for everyone, but most of us miss her dearly. You're her nephew then?"

"Great nephew." He stuck his hand out. "Griffin Carpenter."

She shook it, still smiling. "Nice to meet you, Griffin. I'm Kelly Singh. I'm the editor of the Gazette. I'm also its main reporter. And I make the coffee." With a laugh, she gestured to the chair in front of her desk. "Have a seat, please."

He did as she asked, setting his portfolio across his knees.

She took her chair, too. "How long have you lived in Blackbird Beach?"

Gulf Coast Secrets

He looked at his watch. "About fourteen hours."

She laughed. "Pretty sure that makes you our newest citizen."

"I'm happy to be here. With my family."

"So you'll be staying then?"

He thought about what she'd told him, about the other photographer getting a better offer in a bigger city. She had to be wondering about that. "Absolutely. I'm going to shoot the weddings at the inn, and I hope to set up my studio here eventually."

"That's good to hear." She glanced at the book on his lap. "Is that your portfolio?"

He nodded and held it out to her. "Would you like to see it?"

"I would." She took it and opened it up, then put her glasses back on her face. She flipped through a few pages without saying a word.

He didn't know if that was bad or good. Should he try to sell himself a little more or let her keep looking? He didn't have to decide.

"I'm impressed." She raised her head. "You're really good. Probably too good for our little newspaper."

"Thank you, that's very kind of you, but I don't think that's true that I'm too good. I'd say I'm just good enough. I promise I can get whatever shot is required for the job. Whether that's a beautiful bride or a high school quarterback making the winning pass." He shrugged. "Or even the blue-ribbon pie at the fair."

She smiled. "I like that attitude very much. You should know that this job isn't full time, unfortunately. I'm the only full-time employee. Everyone else is part-time, which is what the photographer's job is since we'd only need you when there was an event going on. Is that something you'd be all right with?"

He nodded. "Absolutely. Doing this kind of work will help me build my portfolio and get my name out there. I'm fine with that."

"Okay, then." She looked at a few more photos then closed the portfolio. "You've got the job. Let's talk pay."

"There is one other thing I should tell you first."

"Oh?"

"I have an infant daughter. I may have to bring her with me on some of the shoots. Especially when my mom and sister get busier with running the inn. I hope that won't be a problem." It had gotten him fired from his last shoot. He didn't want to go through that again. Chloe was his first priority.

Kelly shook her head. "We're a small paper. In a small town. If we didn't understand the importance of family and how it can impact our daily lives, we probably wouldn't be around anymore. It's not a problem."

He exhaled. "Thank you. Now about that pay…"

By the time Griffin headed back to the inn, his entire mood had changed. He'd gone from the low point of feeling a soul-deep desperation to feeling like his footing was firm again.

Amazing what having a job could do for a guy. Kelly had been pretty good for his confidence, too. She'd praised his portfolio a few more times before he'd left, prompting him to offer her a free photo session.

Gulf Coast Secrets

She taken him up on it so fast that he could only believe she meant what she'd said about his work.

Nice to have a boss who appreciated him. And didn't have any issues with Chloe coming along with him.

The only issue was the pay. Or the lack thereof. He got it. Being the paper's photographer was a part time job. He couldn't expect that kind of work to make him financially independent overnight. But unless he got a second job, there was no way he would be able to afford a place for him and Chloe any time soon.

He knew that meant he had more looking to do, and he definitely would, but first he wanted to check on his daughter and see how she was doing. Today was the first time in two weeks that they'd been apart for any length of time and it surprised him how much he missed her already.

He parked in front of the inn and went inside. The place was beautiful. He could imagine doing photo shoots there, from high fashion stuff to weddings. Anything really. He looked around for a second more, but he was too desperate to see Chloe to do any further inspection of the place.

"Mom?"

"Back here," she called out.

He didn't really know where back here was, but he walked toward the direction of her voice through the long living room area. He found her and Mia and another man, who he assumed was Travis, the handyman, in the kitchen painting away.

His mom smiled at him. "How did it go at the paper?"

He smiled back. "I got the job."

"That's fantastic," Mia said.

He nodded. "It really is. Thanks, Mom. I owe you. I'd never have known if you hadn't told me."

"Thank Travis," she said, looking over at the other man, who was up on a ladder. "He's the one who knew about it. Griffin, meet Travis Taylor, the inn's resident handyman."

"Very nice to meet you." Griffin walked over to him. "And thank you, sir. I really appreciate the tip."

Travis climbed down. "Happy to help. And you don't need to call me sir." He put his hand out. "Travis will do."

Griffin shook the man's hand. "Pleased to meet you, Travis."

"You too, Griffin. Your mom has said a lot of nice things about you."

Griffin laughed. "She's required to say all that by law, I think."

Travis nodded. "Yeah, that's how moms are."

He looked back at his mom. "Where's Chloe? I just want to see her for a couple minutes, then I'm going to head back out and see if I can find a second job."

Travis's brows shot up. "You are a hard worker."

"Well," Griffin said. "I have a daughter to provide for."

Travis smiled and glanced at Georgia. "The offer still stands."

Griffin didn't know what that meant but before he could ask, Mia spoke up.

"Chloe's in the breakfast room right next door." She pointed to the door a few feet away.

"Thanks." He went through it immediately.

Chloe was laying in a crib, her stuffed giraffe next to her.

Gulf Coast Secrets

He smiled at her, all right in his world at the sight of her. "Hello, sweetheart. How's my baby girl?"

She gurgled and made grabby hands at him.

He picked her up and put her against his chest, instantly calmed by the contact. He closed his eyes and rocked her gently back and forth. "Daddy got a job, Chloe. And you might be tagging along. What do you think of that?"

He walked over to the French doors that looked out to the deck and the beach beyond. There was something about seeing all that calm blue water out there that made him think things were going to be okay. It was so peaceful.

More than that, this felt like home already. And maybe it was the place or maybe it was having his family around him, but suddenly the enormous burden of being a dad felt bearable.

He kissed Chloe's downy little head and whispered, "We're going to be all right, Chloe girl. Just you wait and see."

Maggie Miller

Gulf Coast Secrets

Chapter Five

Georgia realized that in the rush to get ready this morning, she'd never called Roger Gillum like she'd meant to. "Travis? I need to take a minute and make a phone call. I'll be right back."

"Sure thing," Travis said.

She put her roller down in the paint tray and walked through the inn towards the front where she could have a little more privacy. As she went, she dialed Roger's number.

His receptionist answered. "Good morning. Roger Gillum's office. How may I help you?"

"Hi, Flora. It's Georgia Carpenter. May I speak with Mr. Gillum please?"

"Absolutely. Just a moment, Ms. Carpenter."

Soft jazz began to play on the line as Georgia was put on hold. A few seconds later, Roger answered.

"Good morning, Ms. Carpenter. What can I do for you today?"

Maggie Miller

"Good morning, Mr. Gillum. I was calling for two reasons. One to see how things were going with my almost ex-husband and his claim against the inn."

Roger responded quickly. "I have a letter drafted that I'll be sending out today. I've explained in full detail that he has no claim to your inheritance. I'd be surprised if they make any further attempts after this, but I don't know how quickly we'll hear back."

Georgia sighed in relief. "That's fine. Thank you so much. I hope you're right, I hope this is the end of it."

"I promise you if they come back again, I will file a counterclaim against them. Which I mentioned in the letter. I will not let him take any piece of this property."

"Excellent." Georgia smiled. Roger Gillum was a good man to have on her side. "The other thing I wanted to ask you about is a little more complicated. My son has decided to move here, and he's brought his infant daughter with him. She's the reason I'm calling."

"Oh?"

"I'm not going to lie. It's a strange situation. The baby, Chloe, was left on his doorstep with a note. He did a paternity test, and she is definitely his, but he's not entirely positive who the mother is, although he has a good idea. But he's got no birth certificate for her. And no clue of her exact birthdate. Right now, that might not be a big deal, but it's going to make things tricky in the future."

"It will indeed."

"I'm also concerned about the mother coming after her. Griffin is clearly enamored with his baby daughter. It would devastate him to lose her. Is there anything you can do to make sure he has full custody of her?"

"Hmm." Gillum hesitated like he was thinking. "If the mother left the baby on your son's doorstep, in his care, that sets a precedent, but courts often rule in the mother's favor regardless. I'll need some further information like the mother's name, where your son believes the baby was born, anything like that."

"I'll get you everything I can. Actually, would it be okay if I sent my son to see you? I know your time isn't free but I'm happy to pay for it."

"That would be fine. I'll make sure I see him when he arrives."

"Thank you. For everything."

"You're very welcome, Ms. Carpenter. How's the inn coming?"

She smiled. "Good. We're painting inside today. Which I should probably get back to. We're shooting to be open sometime in December."

"Outstanding. I'll let you get back to it, then. Have a good day."

"You too." She hung up just as Griffin was headed toward her. "Going back out to do some more job hunting?"

He nodded. "I am."

"Well, I need you to do something else first. Go see my attorney, Roger Gillum, and give him as much information as you can about the woman you think might be Chloe's mother. He's going to help us make sure you have full custody of her."

"Really? That would be amazing." He exhaled. "I'm not going to lie. The thought of Olivia taking her back has been on my mind a lot."

Georgia wondered if that wasn't part of his motivation to move here. "I'll text you Roger's address. He's waiting to see you." She already had her phone in her hands, so she pulled up the office information and forwarded it to Griffin.

His phone chimed. "I'll go immediately."

"Thanks."

He kissed her cheek. "Thank you. Love you."

"Love you too. Oh! One more thing. Travis lives in a cottage just like the one Mia and I are in. He's offered his second bedroom to you and Chloe."

Griffin's mouth hung open. "Really? That's a pretty major thing to do."

Georgia nodded. "It is, but he's a good man with a kind heart. Think about it, okay?"

"I will." He held up his phone. "Off to see the lawyer. Then hopefully find job number two."

She smiled. "Go get 'em, tiger."

He left and she went back to the kitchen but took the long way through the breakfast room so she could check on Chloe. She was fast asleep. How long that would last there was no telling, but Georgia knew it was a good opportunity to get busy. When Chloe woke up, she'd need a diaper change and a bottle.

She hurried back to the kitchen to find Mia painting one wall and Travis climbing down the ladder.

"I'm going to run upstairs and see how the grout is drying," he said. "Won't be long."

Gulf Coast Secrets

"No problem." She picked up her roller and got back to work. The soft yellow she and Travis had picked out was really beautiful in the space. The perfect buttery color for a big kitchen. And when they had the new lighting and new floor installed, it would be even better.

She really wanted to put new hardware on the cabinets too, but she'd priced out what she liked, and it was a little too rich for her current budget. Even the simplest of knobs and pulls were a lot of money, mostly because the kitchen was so large and there were so many cabinets to redo.

It wasn't an area the guests would see so this was really for herself and Mia and whoever they hired as their cook. Which was probably something they needed to be thinking about. There was a lot to be thinking about, actually.

She glanced over at her daughter. "Have you dug into Aunt Norma's records yet to see what she charged? We need to figure out how we're going to price the rooms."

Mia answered as she dipped her roller in paint again. "Not really. I was thinking I would find out what other inns and B&Bs nearby are charging and make sure we're competitive. We obviously can't operate at a loss, but if we can keep our prices a little lower initially, it might help. If you're okay with that."

"I might be. It depends on how the letter writing campaign goes. Which we should probably get to work on." Mia had come up with the idea of writing to all the most recent past guests and offering them a special return rate if they would like to come and stay at the Sea Glass Inn again. Georgia had immediately agreed. It was a great idea.

Maggie Miller

A lot of those guests had been repeat visitors anyway. Why wouldn't they want to come and stay again? At least that was what Georgia and Mia were banking on.

"Agreed," Mia said. "I should take some of the guest books home and get to work on them." She stopped and shook her head. "Actually I won't need to, if we're going to move over here tomorrow."

"Well," Georgia said. "It's going to take us a day at least. Not that we have that much stuff, but we need to pack it up and haul it over here. And then unpack again. Do you want to work on that tomorrow?"

Mia looked around the room. "Only if we get this kitchen done. That's got to be our priority. Living in a place without a usable kitchen will make things a little trickier. Let's see how long the painting takes us. Then worry about moving over here."

"Fine with me."

In the other room, Chloe started to cry. Mia and Georgia looked towards the sound immediately.

Mia put her roller down. "I can go get her."

"She's going to need a diaper change and a bottle," Georgia said.

"I can handle it. Unless you want to get the bottle ready?"

"Sure." Georgia was surprised Mia hadn't asked her to handle the diaper change. Pleasantly surprised. Georgia set her roller down as well and got to work on the bottle.

Between them, they got Chloe changed and fed before she cried for too long. Then Georgia threw a burp cloth over her shoulder, put Chloe on it and walked her around the house, patting her softly on the back.

Gulf Coast Secrets

"Look at this pretty house, Chloe. What do you think? Would you come stay here?"

Chloe's response was one small burp.

"You can do better than that." Georgia headed back toward the breakfast room and stood by the French doors. "I can't wait to take you to the beach. You're going to love it. Your daddy was always a water baby. I wonder if you will be too?"

Another longer burp was the only answer Georgia got.

"Good girl." She walked with Chloe a little more, patting her back and talking to her, but there was nothing else in her but a soft sigh.

Georgia took her back to the crib and set her down gently. Chloe's lids looked heavy, so Georgia sang her a soft lullaby until they closed all the way. Then she straightened, smiling. What an angel. There was nothing she wouldn't do to protect this child.

"Nicely done, Mimi."

She looked up to see Travis was back downstairs. She smiled. "I had plenty of practice with my own two."

There was a wistfulness in his eyes that made her realize he had to be thinking about all the years he'd missed with his grandson, Clayton, a child Travis hadn't seen since Clayton's birth nine years ago.

"You want to hold her?" Georgia asked.

He shook his head quickly. "She's sleeping."

"Next time she's awake?"

Travis stared into the crib, the pain in his eyes unmistakable. "Maybe." He looked up. "I mean, if she and

Griffin are going to move in with me, she might as well get used to me, right?"

"Right." Georgia realized right then what a sacrifice Travis was making for them. Offering up his home wasn't just giving up his personal space. It was allowing into his home a constant reminder of what he'd missed out on.

Georgia's heart hurt for him. But maybe being a part of Chloe's life would be good for him. She hoped so. Travis deserved some happiness in his life. Even if it wasn't from his own family.

Chapter Six

Travis wasn't the kind of man to dwell. Once upon a time, maybe. But he'd learned to compartmentalize and get on with his life. Such as it was.

Of course, working for Norma had made that easy. She kept him busy not just with work but with their friendship. Often, after a full day's work, they'd sit together on her private side porch in the evenings, having a bourbon or sometimes a glass of the tart lemonade Norma liked so much. Norma would tell him stories about her amazing, interesting life that never failed to entertain.

And he'd forget about all the pain of his own.

But now as he looked at Chloe, in all her tiny infant perfection, he couldn't help but think about his daughter Sam and the child she'd had so early in life. Clayton, his grandson. He'd only seen the boy once, right after he'd been born.

After that, Travis's wife Jillian, had made things miserable. She'd decided there was more to life than being married to

Maggie Miller

Travis. She and Sam and Clayton had picked up and moved to Alabama. Jillian had also turned Sam against him.

Because of that, Travis hadn't really talked to his daughter in the nine years that she'd been gone. She wouldn't call him, wouldn't answer his calls or his text messages. Jillian was a brick wall too.

Not that he'd expected differently from her.

He'd sent Clayton a birthday present every year, but he didn't have a clue if the boy had gotten any of them. Now, all Travis could do was hope for a glimpse of his grandson on Facebook. And those didn't begin to be enough. All they did was make Travis's heart ache more for all the time that had been lost.

Was it weird of him to wonder if he could fill the role of grandfather for Chloe? Obviously, he wasn't her family. But having been so close to Norma for so long, he'd allowed himself to think of himself as part of her family.

Now that Norma's family was actually here and taking over the inn, he knew that things were different. Which wasn't to say Georgia and her daughter weren't wonderful people. They were. It was easy to see why Norma had left everything to Georgia.

But he was back to being Travis, the handyman. Would that change? Maybe, someday. But he didn't want to overreach. Didn't want to assume.

His offer for Griffin and Chloe to stay with him had been spontaneous and maybe he should have thought it over a little more. But it had come from his heart, from the desire to help the family of the woman who had so greatly befriended him.

"We should get back to work," Georgia said softly.

Gulf Coast Secrets

He nodded. "Yep." Work was good. Work kept the mind busy and a busy mind couldn't dwell on what ifs and what should have beens.

As he started for the kitchen, someone knocked at the door. He looked at Georgia. "Want me to get it?"

"Sure. Thanks." She looked down at Chloe. "Didn't wake her up, thankfully."

"Good." He hustled to see who it was before they knocked again and woke the princess. He opened it and found a guy on the porch wearing a Beachside Air and Heat shirt. Another one stood on the walkway. "Hey, Jimmy. Here to run the system check on the AC?"

"Hey, Travis." The guy nodded. "Yep, here for the system check."

He was early, but Travis didn't mind. "It's right around the side. We're in here painting so text if you need me. We also have a sleeping infant in here."

"Okay, no problem. Thanks." He took off around toward the AC units.

Travis shut the door and went back to work. Mia and Georgia were hard at it, almost finished with the biggest wall. "You guys are making great progress."

"Thanks," Mia said. "Who was at the door?"

"HVAC guys here to check the system."

"Fingers crossed," Georgia said.

Half an hour later, the Beachside Air and Heating guys were back. And with a decently good report. Travis nodded as he looked over the invoice. "That was a lot of freon."

"You had a small leak, which we fixed too."

"I see that. All right, let me go get you a check." He closed the door and returned to the kitchen. "Good news or bad news?"

Georgia grimaced. "Bad news first. I guess."

"The system had a leak."

"Oh no," Mia said. "That has to be bad."

Travis smiled. "It's not great but it's a lot better than what could have been. The good news is they fixed it, recharged the freon and we're good to go." He held up the invoice. "And the bill isn't too terrible. But they do need a check."

Georgia stopped painting and went for her purse. "I'm on it." She grabbed her checkbook and came over to him, looking at the paper for the figure. A decent sum, but nothing that would break the budget. "Hey, you're right. That's not too terrible after all. What a relief."

She scribbled off a check and handed it to him.

He ran it back to the workers and when he returned to the kitchen, he found that Georgia and Mia were cleaning up. "Lunch?"

They nodded.

Mia glanced toward where Chloe was sleeping. "We'll go make sandwiches if you keep an eye on her."

He smiled. "I'd be happy to do that."

"Ham and cheese on wheat okay?"

"Perfect."

"Mayo or mustard?" Mia asked.

He looked at Chloe, still smiling. "Surprise me."

"Cool," she said. "We'll be back in a bit."

"Sounds good." He went back to painting, his smile stuck in place. It made him happy that they trusted him to watch

Gulf Coast Secrets

Chloe. Of course, they wouldn't be gone long. What did it take to make a few sandwiches? Ten minutes? Fifteen at most?

Didn't matter. It made him feel good. He kicked his efforts into overdrive and finished the big wall, setting the roller down as they returned.

They spread out lunch on the big six top table in the breakfast room. Ham and cheese sandwiches, pickles, a bag of Ludlow's potato chips, three apples, and three bottles of water. They were about halfway through when Chloe woke up again, whimpering softly.

Travis got up. "I've got her. You two finish your lunch."

He picked her up carefully, reminded instantly of Sam as a baby, and cradled her in his arms. "Hiya, princess," he said softly. "How was your nap?"

She sniffled, staring up at him with the most beautiful eyes.

He made a silly face and was rewarded with big eyes from her, then a laugh. He looked back at Georgia. "Is that not the best sound in the world?"

She smiled. "It really is. You're pretty good at that."

He looked down at Chloe. "She's an easy baby. Aren't you? Yes, you are."

Mia snorted. "There's something both sweet and hilarious about a guy like you talking baby talk."

"Well, get used to it," he said. "Because with this princess around, you're going to be hearing a lot more of it."

Chloe blew a bubble and smiled at him.

In that moment, Travis felt a lightness of spirit he hadn't felt in nine years. A feeling like part of his wounded soul wasn't quite so wounded anymore. It was remarkable really, but looking into Chloe's face, nothing seemed impossible.

He'd felt the same way when he'd first held Sam. Babies had a way of reminding you about all the things that were good and right in the world, and after losing Norma, it was good to feel that way again.

"Thanks, princess," he whispered.

Gulf Coast Secrets

Chapter Seven

After the good news about Griffin getting a job and the air conditioning bill being less than expected, Georgia was in the mood to celebrate. As she painted, an idea came to her. "Let's have dinner on the back deck again. Our place."

"Yeah?" Mia looked down from her position on the step ladder. She was painting above the cabinets, a slow and tricky process. "I'm in. What do you want to have?"

"Something easy. A cookout. Burgers and hotdogs?"

"That actually sounds pretty good." Mia looked over at Travis, who was stirring the big bucket of paint before refilling their trays. "What do you think?"

His brows went up. "Are you inviting me?"

"Yes," Georgia said. "Don't be silly."

He shrugged but smiled. "I will never turn down burgers and hotdogs. What can I bring? You want me to get another chocolate silk pie from Ludlow's?"

"Key lime is on sale this week," Mia said. "I'd be all right with one of those."

"So would I," he said. "I'll go grab one after we're done here. What about buns? Chips? Some kind of side dish? Tell me what else you need, and I'll get it. No point in making more than one trip."

"Thanks," Georgia said. "I'll make up a little list. Now, what do you say we crack on and get this room done? Please? We're so close."

"We are," Travis said. "But we have the more tedious painting to do around the cabinets and that's just naturally going to take longer. Still, we should be able to get it done. Most of it anyway. Which reminds me, Diego texted earlier. They're going to start work on the exterior tomorrow."

"Excellent," Georgia said. Diego was the painting contractor who would be repairing and repainting the exterior stucco and trim. He was going to do the little fence at the front of the property as well.

"Yay!" Mia grinned. "This place is going to look amazing after it's painted, and all the trim is fresh and white again. I can't wait."

"It will finally look like it's supposed to after so long," he answered.

"Mia?" Georgia asked. "Did you get before pictures? To post on Instagram?" Mia had started an Instagram and a Facebook account for the inn and was documenting the rehab project with the idea of generating interest in potential guests.

She nodded. "I got a few but I'm going to ask Griffin to get some first thing in the morning before they put up any scaffolding. I know his will be better."

"That's great. Thanks, kiddo."

Gulf Coast Secrets

They got back to work, falling silent as they focused on finishing. Travis had been right, though, Georgia thought. Painting around cabinets was a lot more work than painting a big blank wall. Even so, they went at it with their full concentration, only taking a few breaks to tend to Chloe and get drinks.

It was easy to see time pass as the light outside faded.

With a sigh, Georgia wiped her arm across her forehead. "Okay, I'm calling it. We're close but we can knock out the rest tomorrow. Then Mia and I can work on starting the move over. What do you say?"

Travis nodded. "Sounds good. There's no reason to rush that move either. I mean, if it takes one day or three days, it's not like you're on a deadline."

"No. But it would be nice to get it taken care of," Georgia said. Was he thinking that their move would mean Griffin and Chloe would be bunking with him sooner than expected? Was he regretting it?

She hoped not. But then again, it was his home. His decision to make. If he'd changed his mind about the offer—

"Don't forget my second bedroom doesn't need any work. It's ready for Griffin and Chloe whenever they are. In fact, maybe we should move them to my place tomorrow. That would be the easiest thing to get done. Then we can focus on you and Mia."

Well, that answered that. She smiled. "Let's see what Griffin says at dinner tonight."

"Okay." Travis glanced at Mia. "How about you and I start the clean up so your mom can make a grocery list?"

"Sure thing," Mia said.

Maggie Miller

Georgia went to her purse for a pen and piece of paper. "It won't take me long. We don't need much." She started jotting down the things they'd need for the cookout and it occurred to her that she hadn't heard anything from Griffin since he'd been by to see Chloe.

She didn't know if that was good news or bad news, but even if he hadn't found another job, he still had the one at the paper. And they could certainly use more help around here. Not just with the moving.

They hadn't even started the cleaning that needed to be done. Even with the drop cloths that had been used to cover most of the upholstered furniture, there still seemed to be a layer of dust on everything.

The massive blown glass and crystal octopus chandelier in the foyer might take a day to clean all by itself.

From base boards to crown moldings and everything in between, the inn required a deep cleaning. There were salt-crusted windows to wash outside, furniture to polish, mirrors and glass to clean, walls to wipe down, rugs to vacuum and possibly shampoo, curtains and bed linens to wash or replace, rooms to be aired out, bathrooms to scrub, walls to touch up with paint…it was an exhausting list.

And she hadn't even begun to calculate the things that needed to be purchased, like all new furniture for the back deck. And any curtains or bed linens that needed to be replaced. There was a pantry to restock, too.

Which made her think again about the cook she'd need to hire, as well as at least one housekeeper.

She sighed.

"You okay," Travis asked.

She looked over at him and nodded. "Just feeling a little overwhelmed is all."

"Where's your list?"

She held up the scrap of paper she was writing on. "Working on it."

"No, the To Do list you made with all of the things we needed to accomplish to get the inn open again."

"Oh." She thought a moment. "It's stuck to the fridge back at the cottage."

"You want to go over it again tonight? Reassess? Make sure you've got everything?"

She nodded. "Yes, I think that would help."

He put his hand on her arm for the briefest of moments. "I know this is a massive project and I'm sure you're stressed about it, but you're not doing it alone."

She smiled. "No, you're right. I'm not."

The inn's front door opened.

"Mom?"

"Back here, Griff."

He walked into the kitchen, his tie loosened and a slightly defeated look on his face. "How's my girl?"

"Still perfect."

That earned her a hint of a smile. "I'm surprised you guys are still here."

"Packing up now," she said. "But we're going to have a cookout at the cottage for dinner." She smiled. "The HVAC bill was a lot less than expected and you got a job. That's worth celebrating."

He nodded but still looked a bit down.

Maggie Miller

All of her mom instincts went into overdrive. "What's wrong? Something's wrong, I can tell. Is this about finding work or the meeting you had with Mr. Gillum?"

He hesitated. "I didn't find another job. As for my meeting with the lawyer, can we talk about it later?"

"Sure. But is it good or bad?"

"I don't know yet."

She decided something right then and there. "I'm glad you didn't find another job."

He frowned. "You are?"

"I could really use you here. And I'm not asking you to volunteer. I'll pay you an hourly wage, same as I pay your sister."

"Really?"

"Hey," Mia said. "I'm getting paid for this?"

Georgia laughed. "You are now. It's not fair to ask you both to help without paying you. This is a lot of work and you have bills." She looked at Griffin. "So what do you think? Are you interested?"

He grinned. "Heck, yes, I'm interested. What do you need me to do?"

"Nothing right now, not in your nice clothes anyway. Actually, that's not true. You can take Chloe home while we finish cleaning up."

His grin widened. "That I can do. I was going to give her a bath tonight so I'll do that as soon as we get in."

Georgia's whole being lightened up. "Could you wait until I get there? I would love to help with that."

"Absolutely. Bathing a baby is surprisingly scary the first time you do it."

She nodded. "You'll get the hang of it."

"I'm sure I will, but I still wouldn't mind the help, so I'll wait for you. I need to wash her clothes, too, so I'll throw a load in first. I don't have a lot of stuff for her."

"Sounds good. Mia and I won't be long. Travis is going to run to the store and get everything we need. Say…have you thought about his offer?"

"I have and I'm going to accept. It's the best possible solution so you can get the cottage rented out."

Travis joined them. "Did I hear you say you're going to be my new roommate?"

Griffin nodded. "You did. I want to say I'm really grateful for the offer and very appreciative. You're taking a lot on to invite a baby into your house."

Travis smiled. "I'm looking forward to it. Place is entirely too quiet."

Griffin barked out a laugh. "Chloe will solve that for you."

"I have no doubt, but I'm ready for it. We'll get you moved in tomorrow afternoon, then, what do you say?"

"All right. Thank you." Griffin looked at his mom. "I'm going to get Chloe and I'll see you back at the cottage."

"Okay," she said. As he left, she reached out and squeezed Travis's hand. "Thank you again."

"Happy to do. Even in that small cottage it gets a little lonely. It'll be nice having company for a while."

All she could hope was that he didn't change his mind if that company kept him up at night.

Maggie Miller

Chapter Eight

Mia hadn't intentionally been eavesdropping, but she'd heard her brother say that he didn't have a lot of clothes for Chloe. The moment those words were out of his mouth an idea popped into her head.

On her way into the laundry room to wash up, she found Travis already at the sink scrubbing the paint specks off his hands. "Hey, do you mind if I tag along to Ludlow's with you?"

"Sure thing," he said. "Does that mean we can use your employee discount card?"

"Absolutely. There's just one little errand I need to run first when we get there, then I'll come back and find you in the store."

He gave her a curious look.

"No, this isn't about Lucas," she said. Lucas Ludlow was the store manager and the son of the man who owned the grocery. He'd basically gotten her the job. He was also a couple years older than Mia, single, and very interested in taking her out for coffee.

Travis laughed softly. "I wasn't judging. Do you need me to take you somewhere else?"

"Nope." She returned his look with a sly smile. "Just to Ludlow's. I can handle the rest from there."

"Okay." He shook his hands dry. "I'll wait for you."

"Thanks." With the same smile still on her face, she went to work getting herself cleaned up. She had some paint splatters on her hands and arms, which probably meant she had some in her hair and on her face too. But she could do that washing up later. Right now she had an errand to run and she wanted to do it before it got too late.

She finished scrubbing and went back out to see how things were going. "Are we almost done?"

Travis was setting the brushes to dry on top of the big five-gallon bucket of paint. "I'd say we are. There's no need to pull everything down since we haven't finished yet."

"Then let's go. We've worked long enough today."

Georgia grabbed her purse. "No argument from me. Not when I get to go home and help give Chloe a bath."

"Mom, I'm going to Ludlow's with Travis so we can use my employee discount, then I'll be home."

"Oh, good, we need creamer and I forgot to put it on the list."

"I'll get it." As her mom left, Mia helped Travis turn off the lights and lock up. They walked down the porch steps and to his cottage where his truck was.

He unlocked it and they got in. As he started up the engine, he looked at her. "Come on, what's this errand you have to

Gulf Coast Secrets

run? It's not something that's going to make your mother mad, is it? Not that I think you'd do something like that, but I do not want to get on her bad side."

"It's nothing bad at all. I promise." Then she shook her head, amused by his curiosity. "I just don't want to jinx it."

He laughed. "Okay."

He backed out and headed to Ludlow's. "You just want me to park in the lot? Or somewhere else?"

"In the lot is fine. I won't be long. And I'll come find you."

"You are just like your aunt. She liked to keep her plans secret too. At least until she'd done whatever it was she'd intended to do."

Mia chuckled. "I am perfectly okay with that. In fact, maybe that's where I get it."

He parked at Ludlow's and they both got out.

She gave him a little wave. "See you inside."

He nodded. "Yep."

She took off across the street to the thrift shop where she'd taken a lot of Aunt Norma's things after cleaning out her bedroom. Bon Voyage Vintage was only open for another half an hour, but she wasn't going to need that much time. The little bell over the door clanged as she went inside.

"Mia!"

She looked toward the sound of her name being called. "Hi, Agatha." Mrs. Goodwin had been a good friend of Aunt Norma's and was the woman in charge of the Methodist church's thrift store. She and her group of friends had all played bridge at the inn with Norma, a meeting Mia hoped to reinstate. "How are you?"

"Just fine. How are things coming along at the inn?"

"Good. Busy as all get out, but that's how you get things done, right?"

"Right." She looked at Mia's hands like she expected to see bags of clothes in them. "What brings you in?"

Mia smiled. "Baby clothes. Have you got any?"

"Oh, yes, tons of them. You know, they grow so fast most of them are like brand new." Then Agatha's brows bent. "You're not expecting, are you?"

"What? No!" Mia laughed. "My brother moved to town with his baby daughter and she's in desperate need of a wardrobe update. My first niece. I want to spoil her a little."

"Oh, a baby! Aren't they just the best? Come on, follow me." Agatha came out from behind the counter and led Mia back to the right-hand side of the shop. It was nothing but baby things. Toys, books, clothes, and anything else a baby might need. "Here you go."

"Wow, look at all this," Mia said.

Agatha nodded. "We're never low on baby things. You should find more than you need in here. I'll let you look. You just give me a hoot if you need me."

"Thanks, I will." Mia started digging through the racks and shelves. It really was a treasure trove. But she was mindful of her time, too. It wasn't going to take Travis long to get the small list of items Georgia had given him.

She selected an armful of the cutest, girliest clothes including several onesies, a zoo animals crib mobile, a play mat, a trio of pacifiers still in the packaging, an activity book, a pair of pink booties, and a lavender knitted headband with kitty ears on it.

Gulf Coast Secrets

She had no idea how much it was all going to cost but she carried it up the front counter where Agatha was waiting. "I'm ready."

"Oh, aren't these cute?" Agatha picked up the booties. "You got all the best things." She started bagging everything up.

Mia took her wallet out of her purse as she waited for the total.

Agatha handed her two very full bags. "Here you go."

Mia held up her wallet. "How much?"

"Put that away." Agatha shook her head. "Honey, you brought us more than enough of your aunt's things to compensate for all of this. You just go spoil that niece of yours."

"Really? You're sure?"

"Absolutely."

"That is so nice of you. Thank you." Impulsively, Mia leaned across the counter and hugged Agatha. She smelled like roses.

Agatha giggled and patted her on the back. "You're very welcome. Now, you skedaddle. I have to close up so I can get home in time to watch the Wheel."

Mia laughed. "All right, thanks again." She took off across the street and went straight into Ludlow's.

She found Travis approaching one of the checkout lines. "There you are. Did you remember creamer?"

"I did." He looked at the bags she was carrying. "What's all that?"

"My errand. Some new things for Chloe from Bon Voyage Vintage. Well, not new, exactly. But pretty close."

He smiled as he pushed the cart into the next available lane. "That's very nice of you, Aunt Mia. That little princess deserves to be spoiled."

Mia liked that he called Chloe a princess. It was very sweet. "I heard Griffin say she didn't have many clothes. So…" Mia shrugged.

"You're a good sister. And a good aunt."

"You're all right, yourself. It was pretty nice of you to offer up your spare room." She took a quick look around for Lucas, but she knew he wasn't working. She still found herself disappointed not to see him.

They inched forward in the lane with everyone else shopping for dinner, which wasn't all that many people but for Blackbird Beach it constituted a rush.

Travis picked up a bag of peanut M&Ms from the display. "I'm looking forward to the company. And I'm sure there will be nights I'll miss out on some sleep, but I know it's only temporary." He winked at her as he added the chocolates to the rest of the groceries. "No big deal, right?"

"Right."

They paid, getting a little discount with Mia's employee card, then Travis carried the bags out to the truck while she walked alongside him.

Her stomach rumbled loudly. She put her hand on her belly. "Sorry."

"No apology needed," he said with a grin. "I'm hungry too. Long days really give you an appetite."

"They do." She put her bags in the back seat of the cab then got into the passenger side.

He did the same on his side, then got behind the wheel.

Gulf Coast Secrets

She clicked her seatbelt into place. "You know, I thought waiting tables was hard, and it was, really hard, and all of this stuff we're doing is hard, too, but the reward that's coming makes it not feel that way. If that makes sense."

"Perfect sense." He drove out of the lot, turning toward Sea Glass Lane. "A lot of that comes from being your own boss, too. Which is pretty much what you are now. I know you're technically working for your mom, but someday that inn will be yours. Nothing pays off like sweat equity."

She nodded. "It's a good feeling."

"It is. And it's going to get even better when you see the fruit of your labors."

Something about that made a question pop into her head. "Do you work for other people beside my aunt? Or did you?"

"I didn't when the inn was open and active, but I had to take on other work when she closed things down. She still paid me, but I made her cut my salary way back. Just enough to cover the maintenance on the cottages. Wasn't fair for her to pay me for work she wouldn't let me do."

Once again, Travis proved what an upstanding guy he was.

He glanced over. "Are you asking me because you want to know if I'm going to come back to the Inn full-time?"

"Just curious I guess."

"I'd like to when the budget allows. Which I think will be pretty soon. People loved that inn. No reason for it not to be busy again."

She nodded. "I'd like for you to come back full-time too. I feel safer knowing you're around if something goes wrong. Is that weird?"

Maggie Miller

He smiled. "No. That's nice to know. Hey, you want to learn how to change out a light fixture? We could do that tomorrow after we finish painting in the kitchen."

She grimaced. "That sounds like it involves electricity."

He laughed. "It does, but it's very safe. I promise."

"I'll think about it. That scares me a little."

"The only way to get over a fear is to face it."

She thought about that. "True. But if you get zapped…"

"You'll learn not to do it that way again."

"That's for sure." Her mind turned to former fiancé, Branden and how he'd cheated on her with her best friend, Sarah. Then her mind moved onto to Lucas. He was a nice guy, but was she willing to put her heart on the line a second time? Willing to get zapped a second time?

Part of her wanted to say yes.

And part of her wanted to say never again.

Chapter Nine

Without a baby tub for Chloe, Georgia prepped the sink by cleaning it very well and rinsing it twice to be sure it was free from residue. Then she filled it with a few inches of perfectly warm water and pushed the faucet out of the way. Clyde, who still seemed pretty curious about the baby, watched from the safe distance of a kitchen chair.

"Okay." She nodded at Griffin. "We're all ready."

Griffin had already undressed Chloe and had her wrapped in a towel. He let that drop and carefully lowered her into the water.

She laughed and slapped her hands against the surface, splashing.

"She's definitely going to be a water baby like you were," Georgia said. She supported Chloe's head in one hand. "Aren't you, sweetie? You like that? Is that fun?"

"Good thing we live by the beach then." He took the washcloth, wet it, and added some baby shampoo to it so he could soap her up.

Chloe didn't seem to notice since she was too busy splashing and laughing.

"In fact," Griffin said, "I can't imagine a better place for her to grow up. When I first came here, my main thought was she needed to be around family. We both did. Now, I'm thinking that not only do we get the benefit of having you and Mia around us, but we get to live in this beautiful place, too."

He shook his head as he lathered Chloe's little pink body. "It's kind of overwhelming."

Georgia smiled. "I feel that way too sometimes. I did a lot the first couple of days. I never thought I'd live in a place that other people only get to visit on vacation."

He let Chloe grab one end of the washcloth, which she found endlessly fascinating for some reason, while he used the other end to finish up her bath. "We owe Aunt Norma a debt we can never repay. I wish I'd been able to know her better."

"She would have loved that. And loved getting to know Chloe. For the record, I feel the same way about the debt we owe her. I've been thinking about it a lot. About a way to pay tribute to her. Hasn't quite come to me yet but let me know if you have any ideas."

"I will." He let Chloe play with the washcloth while he rinsed her. "So Aunt Norma hired Travis?"

"She did. He was more than a handyman to her, though. In the days before her move to the nursing home, he was basically her caretaker."

"Wow. That's above and beyond."

"It was. But then I got the sense that they weren't just employer and employee. They were genuinely friends."

Gulf Coast Secrets

Georgia sighed. "I had a lot of guilt about that when I first found out. Not that Travis had taken care of her, but that I hadn't been here for her. That I hadn't come to visit her more often. I was so occupied with my own life."

"With us," he interjected. "Mom, it's not like you weren't genuinely busy. You were raising kids."

"Honey, you and Mia are in your twenties. There's no reason I couldn't have visited in the last few years. Travis said that at the end, she didn't want anyone around but I'm not sure I totally buy that. Doesn't change the fact that I was just like most people. Living in a world that revolved around me."

"You're being too hard on yourself. Grab that towel?"

Georgia got the towel and opened it up, ready for her granddaughter. Maybe he was right. But then again…those feelings were hard to shake.

He rinsed a last little bit of suds off Chloe's back. "Did Aunt Norma ever call you? Ever write? Ever invite you to visit?"

"No, but she shouldn't have had to do that."

"It's a two-way street, Mom. That's all I'm saying." He picked Chloe up and put her into Georgia's arms. "There you go, Chloe girl. All clean. Thankfully, I have one equally clean onesie ready to go."

Georgia let the subject of Aunt Norma go. Chloe was in her arms and that was more than enough to distract her. "Wasn't that a nice bath?" She looked at Griffin. "Did you already start a load of laundry for her?"

"I did. If you want to dry her off, I'll get her into a diaper and that onesie and give her a bottle."

Maggie Miller

A truck pulled up outside. Georgia glanced through the window, then held Chloe up so she could see better. "Look, there's your Auntie Mia. And Mr. Travis."

"That didn't take them long," Griffin said.

"Ludlow's isn't far."

He nodded. "I know. It's right across the street from the Gazette's office."

She hugged Chloe and bounced her as the baby grabbed at her hair. "When's your first job with them?"

"I'm not sure. I'm supposed to call in every morning to see if there's anything. Otherwise, if something pops up, she'll call me." He held out his hands for Chloe. "Come on, missy. Let's get you dressed."

Mia and Travis came in. Travis had a couple Ludlow's bags. But Mia had bags too.

Georgia turned Chloe over to Griffin then put her hands on her hips. "That looks like a lot more than what was on my list."

"My bags aren't food," Mia said. She put them on the kitchen table and smiled at her brother. "These are for Chloe."

"What is it?" Griffin asked.

She started pulling things out. "Clothes and some other stuff I thought you could use."

"Mia," Griffin started. "That's very generous. And much needed. But it had to cost a ton. You didn't have to spend all that money on her."

Mia grinned. "You can thank Aunt Norma. This stuff didn't cost me anything. For one thing, it all came from the Methodist Church's thrift shop."

Gulf Coast Secrets

"Bon Voyage Vintage," he said. "It's right next door to the Blackbird Gazette."

"Yep."

"But it's a thrift shop, not a charity."

"I took a ton of Aunt Norma's old clothes, shoes, and purses in there to donate them and the woman who runs the shop, Agatha, was a longtime friend of Aunt Norma's and super nice, and anyway, she wouldn't let me pay for any of this. Said the stuff I'd already brought in more than made us equal."

"How about that. Thank you for thinking of her." He smiled at Chloe. "You hit the jackpot, kiddo. Look at all that stuff." He turned his smile on Mia. "Thanks, sis. It's all going to be put to good use, I promise."

"I know it will be." She looked at Chloe. "You're going to be the most spoiled baby in all of Blackbird Beach."

Travis put his bags on the counter and started unpacking them as he spoke to Georgia. "I got everything on the list. Plus some."

She reached for her purse. "What do I owe you?"

"Don't worry about it."

"Travis." She gave him a stern look.

He laughed. "There's a few things in here for me. And I'm eating some of this dinner, so—"

"How much?"

He gave her a stern but amused look right back. "How about we split it?"

Her mouth bent in a half-smile. He was too nice. "I suppose."

Maggie Miller

"Receipts in the bag. I'm going out to start the grill." He took a beer out of the six-pack he'd bought and headed for the outside.

She dug the receipt out, fished out enough cash to cover a little more than half of it, then folded it up to give it to him. Griffin had taken Chloe into the bedroom to dress her.

Mia came over and finished taking the groceries out of the bags. "What can I do to help? You want me to open the packages of burgers and hot dogs?"

"Sure." She put her arm around her daughter's shoulders. "That was a very nice thing you did for your brother."

Mia shrugged, smiling. "How can I not spoil that child? She's perfect and I want to eat her."

Georgia laughed. "I understand that. And you're right, she's going to be incredibly spoiled. And I'm okay with that. She is my first grandchild, after all."

Mia started to unwrap the packages. "Well, enjoy her, because the way I feel, I'm not going to be giving you one any time soon."

Georgia opened the bag of chips and dumped them into a big bowl. "I thought you liked the guy at work. Lucas?"

"I do. But do I like him enough to date him? I mean, maybe. Probably. But I don't think I'm ready. Brandon is still too fresh in my mind. I need to get my life on track. Focus on the inn and getting it open. When that's all up and running, maybe then I'll think about dating again."

Georgia nodded. "I think that's wise. It's not like you have a lot of time to devote to a relationship right now anyway."

Gulf Coast Secrets

"Exactly." Mia suddenly started looking through the bags, then went and opened the fridge. "Do we seriously not have any ketchup?"

She straightened. "Rats."

"Go ask Travis. He must have some at his house."

"Okay." Mia started for the back deck.

"Wait, take the burgers and hotdogs."

"Oops, right." She picked up the plate she'd stacked them on and went outside.

As she left, Clyde meowed at Georgia.

"What's the matter, sweet boy?" The words left her mouth as the answer came into her head. "Your dinner! We haven't fed you yet, have we? Sorry about that."

She got a can of food and fixed him a bowl, then put it down next to his water.

He hopped off the chair and went straight for it.

Georgia went back to work on dinner, slicing tomatoes and onions and shredding lettuce for the burgers.

Griffin came in. "Do you think it's okay if I set up the Pack-n-Play outside on the deck? That way Chloe can hang out with us out there."

"Sure, absolutely. Might be a little cool out as the sun goes down."

He picked up the pink booties that were still sitting on the kitchen table, along with a chunky knit cardigan that might have been a little big and a pair of purple leggings. "I'm going to put her in these. That should do the trick."

"They'll be perfect."

He smiled. "I knew coming back here was the right thing to do."

Maggie Miller

He went back to dress Chloe.

Georgia smiled, her heart full of how sweet life was. A grandchild of all things. Her family around her. And a promising second chance at a happy, successful life. She couldn't imagine how things could get better. Except for getting the inn open.

She returned to the food preparations. Sure, there was a lot to be done at the inn, but they were getting there.

The only fly in the ointment was Robert, her cheating husband, trying to take part of her inheritance, but she had faith in Roger Gillum. He seemed sure he could make that claim go away.

And right now, she chose to believe he could.

Chapter Ten

Griffin finished the last bite of his burger and sat back. He'd also had a hotdog and plenty of chips and macaroni salad, too. They'd all eaten well, including his mom and sister, which was a testament to their day of work.

Chloe had fallen asleep in the Pack-n-Play. Clyde was sitting next to it, looking very much like he wanted to jump in and join her.

Griffin had never really been a cat guy, but there was something sweet about how patient the big orange beast was around her. He couldn't help but think it would be nice for Chloe to have an animal around. Especially one so nice as Clyde.

"I love a cookout. Even a simple one," Georgia said. She put her hands on the table and stood. "But the best part is dessert. I'm going in to get us all a slice of key lime pie. Mia, you want to help me?"

"Sure." She got up and they both went inside.

Travis put a hand on his stomach. "I know I shouldn't, but key lime pie is a weakness. Plus Ludlow's makes some pretty good pies. Good cakes too. Really, their whole bakery is dangerous."

"A slice of key lime sounds pretty good." Griffin wiped his mouth, then tossed the napkin onto the table. "You know my mom used to bake. Mostly cakes and cupcakes. I don't think she ever did pies. She had a little business going for a while, but this stupid divorce put an end to that."

Travis nodded. "I heard." He sat back. "She sure seems extra happy since you and Chloe showed up."

Griff smiled. "I'm so glad about that. I was pretty sure my mom would be happy but then again, there's always that little voice of doubt that tells you otherwise. Especially when you're showing up in need, you know? And with everything my dad has put her through recently and having to move, well…I wasn't a hundred percent. Not that my mom hasn't done everything for us all of her life, but babies are a lot of work."

"They are." Travis nodded. "But you did something pretty magical for your mom. You made her a grandmother. There was no way she was turning down a chance to be a part of her granddaughter's life."

"I'm really glad I figured that part right." Griffin narrowed his eyes. "You like her, don't you?"

Travis's eyes lit up. "I think Chloe's a sweet child."

Griffin snorted. "I meant my mom."

Travis's smile said he'd understood perfectly. "I know. And I do like her. She's a remarkable woman. But if you're

Gulf Coast Secrets

asking me what my intentions are, they're just to be friends with her. Until she decides she wants something different."

He took a sip of his beer. "Is that what you were asking?"

"Sort of." Griffin was glad Travis liked his mom. She deserved a nice guy in her life and Travis sure checked that box. Griffin glanced at Chloe, who was still sleeping. "I was also kind of wondering if you'd offered me your spare room to sweeten her up."

Travis nodded. "Understandable. But I did it because she was in a tough spot and I was able to help. Yes, part of that is because of how I feel about her. Part of it is…" He shook his head. "Never mind."

"Go on. What were you going to say?"

Travis stared at his empty plate. "Your great aunt was like family to me. I think she thought of me that way too."

"I know she did. My mom told me she left you some of her late husband's sports memorabilia. She wouldn't have done that otherwise."

"I'm sure that's true. I don't mind telling you I feel a little bad having that stuff, though. It should have gone to you."

"No, it's right where it belongs. You clearly were there when she needed you and a great friend to her. I'm happy she left you something."

Travis looked up at him. "Thanks."

"You have kids?"

"One." Travis's tone changed ever so slightly, but Griffin didn't know what to make of that. "A daughter."

"Yeah?" Griffin sat up. "That's cool."

Travis looked away. "Well. It was. She hasn't talked to me in a while. Long story short, she sided with her mom after the divorce."

"That's rough. Sorry about that." Griffin instantly felt bad for the guy. What a hard situation. Fortunately for him and Mia, they hadn't gone through any kind of parental battle. For one thing, they were already living on their own.

For another, their father hadn't cared enough to try.

Travis sighed. "Thanks."

The slider opened and Mia and Georgia came back out, carrying two plates each.

Mia set one down in front of Griffin. "Everyone got whipped cream. If you don't want it, scrape it off."

"No complaints," Travis said as Georgia gave him a plate.

"Not from me either," Griffin answered.

They started eating and at the first bite, there were a lot of satisfied sounds.

Mia pointed at her pie with her fork. "This might be as good as the chocolate silk."

Georgia nodded. "I think you're right."

"It is pretty good," Griffin said. The tart lime flavor lingered on his tongue. "But eating it out here, being able to see the water, listening to the sound of the waves and the birds, that might be giving it an unfair advantage."

Mia laughed. "Everything tastes better when you eat it out here. Hey, you want to go for a walk down to the water with me after this?"

"I can't. I have to take Chloe in and put her to bed."

Georgia waved at him. "Um, hello. Her Mimi can do that."

Gulf Coast Secrets

He snorted softly. "Okay." He looked at his sister. "Sure, I'll take a walk with you. I'd like to see the water up close anyway. It looks so glassy."

"It usually is," Travis said. "Of course, not when there's a storm. But even then we don't get the kind of waves they do on the Atlantic side."

Griffin stared out at the beach. "I know I said it already, but I'm surprised not to see anyone paddle boarding."

"They do sometimes," Travis said. "Probably more on weekends. You like paddle boarding?"

Griffin nodded. "Yeah, it's pretty cool. Great way to get out and see the water. I used to give lessons when I was first trying to get my photography going, but I sold my board a while back. I sold a lot of things. I needed the money. But man, I miss it. Maybe when things even out I can get another one."

He looked at Mia. "They don't have any of those at the thrift shop, do they?"

She made her thinking face. "I don't remember seeing one. Agatha would know. I could ask her."

"I was mostly only kidding. I wouldn't think you'd find a paddle board at a thrift shop."

"Why not?" His mom asked. "You never know."

"That would be something. But I can't afford one right now anyway."

Mia suddenly sat up very straight. "Griff. You should give lessons at the inn. To the guests, I mean. Well, obviously. But you could give lessons and we could rent boards and it could be a side business. Or maybe we wouldn't even rent them. Maybe they'd be free for guests to use. Or something like that." She waved her hands around her head. "This all just came to me."

"I love that idea," Georgia said. She turned toward Travis. "Does anyone else do anything like that in town?"

"Not that I'm aware of. You might have to get some kind of extra permit for it. Not sure. And insurance, probably. But yeah, that would be cool. I bet people would love it. Paddle boarding is one of those things that almost anyone can do."

"What about my photography?" But Griffin was already warming to the idea of a little paddle boarding side business. "I don't want to give that up."

"And you shouldn't," his mom said. "But if you could do both…you'd have to keep a good schedule. Not at first, of course. I don't expect any weddings right away, but as things progress."

"Right. I'd have to stay on top of things, I know."

She put her fork down to press her hands together in front of her. "Oh, I love this idea. It's so unique and fun and sounds like the kind of thing that would really appeal to guests. It would set the inn apart, too."

Mia nodded. "Not to mention, a couple shots of Griff shirtless on a paddle board would not be bad for the gram."

"Hey," he said, smiling. "I will not be treated like an object."

She poked him in the shoulder. "I'm the marketing director and you'll do what I say. I promise they'll be tasteful. Just smile and think of the business."

Griffin frowned at her playfully. "When did you get a title?"

"Right now, when I just gave it to myself."

Chuckling, he shook his head. "Mom, you've created a monster."

"Think of Chloe," Mia continued with a teasing smile on her face. "You want her to have nice things, don't you?"

He held his hands up in surrender. "All right, you've worn me down. I'll do it."

"Good," she said. "Now lay off that pie. Bad for the abs."

His mom and Travis broke out in laughter.

Griffin deliberately stabbed another piece of pie. "Hey, I'm a dad now. That means I get to have dad bod."

Mia recoiled in fake horror. "Oh no you don't. Not until I get shots for social media. You can soften up after that."

Griffin rolled his eyes but kept on eating. The idea of doing photography and teaching paddle boarding again was kind of amazing. He'd never thought such an opportunity would come along. Or would even exist, actually.

Not only that, but to do both of those things to help grow his family's business…that was even more amazing.

When the last bite of pie was eaten, Georgia rose to start cleaning up. "You kids go take your walk. I'll look after Chloe and Travis will help me clean up."

Travis nodded. "Yes, ma'am."

"Okay," Griffin said. He didn't need to be told twice. "Thanks."

He and Mia headed down to the beach. "Man, it sure is pretty here."

She stood with her toes at the water's edge. "It really is. And we get to live here."

"I know," he said. "I've been thinking about that. Not sure it's sunk in yet. Granted, I may not live as close as you guys once I eventually find a place, but I'm cool with that."

"I hope you don't move for a while. It's nice having you around. So close, I mean."

"Thanks, kiddo. It all depends on the kind of money I can save and what kind of place I can find. It's going to take me a couple months, at least." He ran a hand through his hair. "I hope Travis is okay with that."

"I'm sure he is, or he wouldn't have offered. He's no dummy."

"No, he isn't." Griffin smiled. "You know he likes Mom."

"I know." Mia smiled too. "I think it's cute. He's the nicest guy. Mom could use a little of that in her life."

"That's for sure."

Mia's smile faded. "She probably hasn't told you but Dad's trying to get a piece of all this. Her inheritance from Aunt Norma, I mean."

Griffin frowned. "Are you serious?"

She nodded. "He called a couple days ago and told her he'd just found out about the inheritance. Wants his share. Like he's even remotely entitled." She shook her head, obviously mad, and stared out at the sea. "I can't believe our father is such a jerk."

"Me either. I've avoided talking to him for a long time." Anger crept up Griff's spine. "But I think that's about to come to an end."

Gulf Coast Secrets

Chapter Eleven

While Travis carried plates in, Georgia carefully picked Chloe up and took her inside and laid her down on Griffin's bed, close to the wall. Chloe couldn't roll over on her own yet, but Georgia wasn't taking any chances.

She went back to the deck and took hold of one end of the Pack-n-Play. It was too cumbersome for her to move by herself. "Travis? Will you help me carry this in?"

He came out. "Sure. Bedroom?"

"Yes."

"Okay."

They picked up their sides and walked it in, setting it against the closet wall, which was the only place for it.

"Thanks," she said.

"No problem. I'll finish bringing the dishes in, then I'm going to clean the grill."

She smiled. "You don't have to do that."

"I don't mind."

Maggie Miller

She picked Chloe up off the bed, thankfully still asleep, and laid her down in the Pack-n-Play. "I know you don't." She straightened and glanced at him. "How did you get to be such a nice guy?"

He laughed softly as he stood beside her looking down at Chloe. "Nice is the kiss of death, isn't it? Nice guys finish last and all that."

"Is that how you feel?"

All traces of humor left his face. "Sometimes." He exhaled. "Sorry. Didn't mean to be a downer. Having this little one around has reminded me of what could have been."

"No need to apologize. It's totally understandable."

"Don't get me wrong. I like having her around. A lot." He smiled again. "Babies are just...a promise. A sign of everything good and right in the world. She gives me hope. She really does."

"She absolutely does," Georgia said. Travis was such a good man. She couldn't stand what his ex had done to him, how she'd turned his daughter against him and made it impossible for him to see his grandson. What kind of terrible person did that? And to a man like Travis, who was as kind and generous as could be?

Georgia's heart filled with such emotion that her impulses took over. She leaned in, planted her hands on Travis's chest, and kissed him.

He kissed her back but a second later, she pulled away. "I shouldn't have—I mean, I didn't, that is...oh, I don't know what I was thinking."

He smiled and held onto her hands, still pressed into his chest. "If you were trying to make me feel better, it worked."

Gulf Coast Secrets

She laughed softly, appreciating his understanding.

Then he cupped her face and kissed her again. The kiss was soft and tender and better than any she'd could remember from her thirty-one years of marriage.

Marriage.

She gasped and pulled away. "I'm technically still married. I shouldn't be kissing anybody."

He let her go and smiled. "I guess I'm crazy because that just makes me like you more."

"Because I'm not available?"

"Because you still care about your vows, despite the other half of your union treating them like they were disposable. You have integrity, Georgia Carpenter. I loved that about your aunt, and I love that about you."

She couldn't help but grin. "Thank you. I suppose it's a little old-fashioned. I'm sure Robert doesn't give a flying fig if I'm kissing someone else. And if he did, that would be pretty ironic. But for some reason, it matters to me. Enough to give me that prickly feeling. You know what I mean?"

He nodded. "I do." He let go of her hands with what seemed like reluctance. "When that divorce is final, how about we go on a date? A real one."

Her smile seemed to be stuck in place. She nodded, maybe a little too enthusiastically. "Okay. That would be nice."

"Good. I'm betting it's been a long time since anyone took you out and treated you the way you should be treated."

He wasn't wrong. And that fact sent a pang through Georgia unlike anything she'd felt in a while. Was that anger? Injustice? Sadness? She wasn't sure. "I think you already know the answer to that."

"I do." He let out a sigh that seemed somewhere between contented and excited. "I should go clean that grill."

She nodded, still a little starry-eyed from the kiss. "And I need to straighten up in the kitchen."

"Meet you on the deck for a drink?"

"Okay. I'll pour myself a glass of wine and bring you a beer."

He looked at her with such intensity she almost couldn't stand it. "Soon, Georgia. As soon as it's final."

And with that, he slipped out the door, leaving her to think about how many years she'd wasted. And how interesting it was going to be making up for all that lost time.

The feeling of all that promise ahead of her left her with the most curious feeling. It was as if she knew she had a gift waiting but couldn't open it yet.

She went into the kitchen and cleaned up what was left of their meal. Which wasn't much. She put the chips back in the bag and clipped it shut, then took care of the few bits of lettuce, onion, and tomato by putting it in a big plastic bag. Pre-made salad for lunch tomorrow. Plenty of buns left, but those could be made into sandwiches.

Nothing would go to waste.

Especially not the glass of wine she was about to pour. She filled it only about half full, however. The evening was already slipping away and like every day to come for a long time, there was too much work to be done tomorrow to face it with a hangover or not enough sleep.

She took a beer with her and joined Travis on the deck.

He was just putting the cover back on the grill.

Gulf Coast Secrets

She handed him the beer. He twisted the top off and lifted it. "Here's to things to come."

A new smile bent her mouth. A simple toast that could mean a thousand different things, but there was only one on her mind at the moment. She clinked her glass against his bottle. "To things to come."

They each took a seat in one of the Adirondack chairs and sat in silence, sipping their drinks and just being.

It was more comfortable than Georgia could have imagined.

About ten minutes after they'd sat, Mia and Griffin walked back up the path from the beach. Griffin looked at Georgia. "Chloe still asleep?"

"Last I checked on her. She's in the Pack-n-Play in your room."

"Okay, thanks." He yawned. "That beach is really something. I can't wait to spend more time out there. But right now, I'm going to bed. I know it's kind of early, but I don't care. I'm beat."

"Me, too," Mia said. "I have my shift at Ludlow's in the morning."

Travis rested his bottle on his knee. "Are we moving anyone tomorrow?"

"The painters are coming, right?" Georgia asked.

He nodded. "Pretty early."

"How early?" Griffin glanced at his sister. "You still want me to take some before pictures?"

She nodded. "I do."

"I'd say by eight," Travis answered. "They'll start putting scaffolding up right away, too."

"Okay, I'll be there in plenty of time." He glanced at his mom. "You can stay with Chloe while I do that?"

"Sure," Georgia answered. "Then when you're done with the pictures, we can take her over there together. Maybe you can help us finish painting?"

"I'd be happy to," Griffin said. "I'll do whatever you need me to do."

"I'm glad you said that, because I think tomorrow we're going to start cleaning." She laughed. "Aren't you glad you offered?"

He shrugged good-naturedly. "Hey, I'm getting paid, right? Put me to work."

"No worries there." Georgia sipped her wine.

Travis's brows went up. "That still doesn't answer my question. Are we moving anyone?"

Georgia swallowed the wine. "I'm going to make an executive decision and say we wait until the inn is done being painted outside. Having to carry all of our stuff in while there's scaffolding up and painting going on…" She shook her head. "Let's just stay focused on our work inside until that job is done."

"All right," Travis said. "Then that's our plan."

Mia wiggled her fingers at them. "And with that, good night."

"Night, kiddo," Georgia said. "Love you. You too, Griff."

"Love you, Mom," they both answered before heading inside.

Travis leaned forward and looked at her. "You're a lucky woman."

Gulf Coast Secrets

She nodded. "I know I am. A month ago, I never thought I'd think that way, but here I am, happier than I've ever been. Life is funny that way, huh?"

"It sure is. I'll see you in the morning, boss."

That made her grin. "In the morning."

He walked home via the beach and she went straight inside. The sounds of her children getting ready for bed were the only things she heard as she did the same herself.

Sleep came quickly too, as it usually did these days.

Crying woke her up. Not quite six A.M. but that was all right. She pulled on her robe and went out to the kitchen. No point in trying to go back to sleep now.

Maggie Miller

Chapter Twelve

Georgia wished she had a camera to capture the moment before her. Griffin sat sleepy-eyed at the kitchen table with Chloe in his arms, giving her a bottle. The scene was sweet and tender and made her see her son in a whole new light. Her boy. A father.

"Morning," she said softly, her heart full.

He nodded and mumbled something.

She smiled and went straight to the coffeemaker and got a pot going. She could hear the shower in the second bathroom turn on. Mia was getting ready for work.

Georgia couldn't help but think how funny it was to have both of her kids back under the same roof with her. Funny in a good way. Funny in a deeply blessed kind of way.

While the coffee brewed, she went back to her room, made her bed, then went to the stacked washer and dryer to check on the last load Griffin had done. Those clothes were the things Mia had brought home from the thrift shop. As suspected, the batch was still in the dryer. Thankfully, the clothes were dry.

She pulled them into the small round basket that had been stored on top of the stacked unit and then took the basket into the kitchen and set it on the table.

"Sorry," Griffin said. "I forgot to do those before I fell asleep."

"Don't worry about it." Georgia started folding the tiny clothes, reveling in the job in a way she never would have suspected. It also gave her a chance to see what all Mia had picked out. Georgia loved the selections.

If there was anything cuter in the world than baby clothes, she didn't know what that was.

When the coffeemaker sputtered and coughed, signaling the coffee was done, she put down the little snap-shouldered pajamas in her hands and went to get a cup. She added two sugars and a splash of cream before putting it in front of her son. "There you go."

"Thanks, Mom." He sighed but his gaze never left Chloe. In fact, he stared down at his daughter like he was cradling an armful of gold.

Georgia went back to folding the remaining clothes. About the time she finished, the shower turned off. Georgia fixed herself a cup of coffee, then went back to her bathroom and took a shower. Clyde was still curled up at the foot of her bed, tail covering his eyes.

The hot water helped wake her up. So did the coffee, which she took into the shower with her. Fortunately, there was a window ledge to set it on safely. She hadn't done that since her own kids had been babies.

Gulf Coast Secrets

Funny how things came full circle.

As she got out she heard crying. Chloe was fussy about something. Georgia wrapped her hair and her body in towels, then went into her bedroom to dig out clothes for the day. Clyde hadn't budged. She wore the same jeans as the day before and a T-shirt she didn't care much about. But it was a good reminder that she'd need to do some laundry of her own this evening.

Dressed, she went back out to get a second cup. The crying hadn't stopped but it was coming from the second bedroom now.

Mia was in the kitchen, dressed in her green Ludlow's shirt and tan pants and already nursing a mug with both hands wrapped around it. Her hair fell in loose, still-damp waves around her face.

"You look sleepy," Georgia said.

"I am." She took a deep breath in and exhaled slowly before answering. "And you were right. That is all."

"About?" Georgia refilled her cup.

Mia sipped her coffee and gave her mother an incredulous look. "About what you hear right now."

"Ah," Georgia said. "Was that going on last night too?"

"Off and on." Mia sighed and shook her head. "It's fine. I'll manage. But yeah, babies aren't great sleepers. At least Chloe isn't just yet."

"She'll get there."

"I know. And I'm fine. I think I said that already." Mia rubbed at her eyes. "Well, I will be fine." She smiled. "Don't say anything to Griffin."

"I won't." The crying had become a kind of repeated sob now.

"Thanks. You need me to bring anything home from the store?"

"No, I think we're good. I was going to make tater tot casserole for dinner."

Mia grinned. "Now that's something to look forward to." She glanced at her watch. "I'd better go. See you later." She drained her mug and put it in the sink. "Hey, will you feed Clyde?"

"Sure thing. Have a good day."

"Thanks, you too." Mia grabbed her purse and her keys and was out the door.

Georgia put a can of food out for the cat, then went back and knocked on the bedroom door. "Griff? Can I help?"

He opened the door, Chloe red-faced in his arms. "I don't know what to do. I've fed her, burped her, changed her…I'm out of ideas. And Mia wants me to take those pictures. I haven't even showered. How did you do this twice?"

Georgia just smiled and held her hands out. "Give her to me."

Without a word of argument, he handed Chloe over.

Georgia gave her granddaughter a big smile. "Good morning, sweet pea. What's the matter? You want to tell Mimi all about it?"

"Maybe you can distract her with Clyde."

"Good idea. Let's go find the kitty, sweet pea." She looked at her son again. "Go shower. I've got it handled."

"Thanks, Mom." He shut the door.

Gulf Coast Secrets

She took Chloe into her bedroom, but Clyde was gone. No where in the room that she could see. Georgia frowned as she bounced Chloe. Where was Clyde? "Where's the kitty, baby girl?"

She took a few steps into the living room but glanced toward his dish. Not there either. That wasn't like him. Usually he was ready for breakfast before coffee was made. "Chloe, you want to help me look for Clyde? The kitty? You want to help Mimi find the kitty?"

Chloe was still sobbing. No wonder Clyde was hiding.

Georgia kept bouncing the baby as she walked through the house, talking in soft, happy tones and calling for Clyde.

The cottage wasn't that big so it didn't take long to do a sweep of it, but unless Clyde was in the bedroom Mia and Griffin were sharing, which Georgia doubted as that had been the epicenter of the crying, he didn't seem to be anywhere.

"Where do you think Clyde went, huh? Where's the kitty, Chloe girl?" Georgia did a loop through the living room then back toward her own bedroom.

Where she saw an orange tail disappear under her bed. She laughed softly.

And Chloe's crying paused.

Georgia laughed again and the little girl blinked at her, making grabby hands. "You like that? How about this?" Georgia let out a low, pretend chuckle.

Chloe waved her hands and gurgled.

"Well, sweet pea, if that's what it takes." Georgia walked into the kitchen, making all the funny laughing sounds she could come up with and after a few more minutes, Chloe settled down and nestled against her shoulder.

Maggie Miller

A little worn out from the effort, Georgia sat in the chair in the living room and gazed out the sliders as the world beyond brightened up. The view of the beach and the water never failed to put her in a calm state of mind.

Minutes ticked by and Chloe was out. Clyde ventured into the living room, peeking around the sofa.

"I know," Georgia said softly to the cat. "Babies are scary, huh? All that noise. Your breakfast is already waiting on you, big man. Better go eat while you can."

She had no doubt the cat was hungry. But she didn't want to risk waking Chloe by trying to take Clyde into the kitchen while holding her, and Griffin had the bedroom door shut so he could get dressed after taking his shower, which meant Georgia couldn't put her down in the Pack-n-Play.

"Go on, follow your nose."

But he came out a little farther from behind the couch and just sat there, watching. Apparently, Chloe was more interesting than the tuna surprise.

The bedroom door opened shortly, and Griffin joined her in the living room. He still looked sleepy. He was in jeans and long sleeve T-shirt, his camera bag slung over one shoulder. "How did you do that?"

Georgia shrugged the shoulder Chloe wasn't resting on. "I laughed, she laughed, and it was all over. Babies are a lot of trial and error. You'll figure it out."

He shook his head. "I hope so. Thank you."

"My pleasure."

"I'm going to shoot these pictures, then I'll be back."

"Take your time. I'm going to put her down in the Pack-n-Play. Then maybe Clyde will eat his breakfast."

Gulf Coast Secrets

"I could use some of that." Griff put his hand on his stomach. "I can wait though. See you in a bit."

"All right, honey." She stayed in the chair until the front door closed, then finally got up and laid Chloe down.

She went back out to the kitchen to make some breakfast when her phone rang. It wasn't even 8 A.M. yet so she couldn't imagine who it was, unless Griffin or Mia had forgotten something.

She looked at the screen. Roger Gillum. She answered quickly. "Good morning, Mr. Gillum."

"Good morning, Ms. Carpenter. I'm sorry to call you so early, but we have a problem."

Maggie Miller

Gulf Coast Secrets

Chapter Thirteen

Griffin was thrilled to be behind the lens again. Despite his tiredness, which was his new normal state of being since Chloe had come into his life, he was energized by having his camera in his hands. He took photos of all sides of the inn, making sure to capture it from many angles so that Mia would have a lot to choose from.

He was almost finished when Travis joined him.

"Morning."

"Morning," Griffin answered.

"My buddy Diego, he's the painter, called to say they were going to be a little late due to a flat tire so you have some extra time if you need it."

"I'm almost done, actually. But I was thinking I might go take a few shots of the beach. This light is too good not to."

Travis nodded. "Mornings are nice around here. Sunsets too."

Maggie Miller

A car pulled up to the curb and a young man got out. He was in dress pants, button down shirt and a tie. He had an envelope in one hand.

Travis turned toward him as he opened the gate and came down the path. "Can I help you?"

"I'm looking for Georgia Carpenter."

Travis shook his head. "She's not here but she will be later. Something I can do for you?"

"I'm her son," Griffin offered. "Maybe I can help?"

The young man held out the envelope. "You can give her this."

Griffin took the envelope. "What is it?"

"Injunction by the town council. Effective immediately, all work on this property must cease."

Griffin wanted to shove the envelope back into his hands. "What the—"

Travis stepped directly in front of the young man. "Did Lavinia send you?"

The young man backed away, headed for his car. "I'm just the messenger."

He scampered away, jumped behind the wheel, and drove off.

Griffin was fuming. "What's the meaning of this? How can they do this? Who's Lavinia?"

Travis stared after the car like he could stop it with sheer willpower. "Norma's archrival, you might say."

"Aunt Norma had enemies?"

"At least that one."

Both Griffin's and Travis's phones started buzzing.

Gulf Coast Secrets

Griffin let his camera hang around his neck so he could pull the phone from the back pocket of his jeans. "Text message."

Travis nodded and read, "Trouble brewing. Gillum's on it."

Griffin shook his head. "I have my pictures. I'm going to take this letter to her. She probably needs to give this to the attorney."

"No doubt." He glanced at the house. "Not sure what to do about the painters."

"Come to the house with me. We can figure it out together."

"Okay," Travis said. "Let's go."

As they started for the house, Griffin put the lens cap back on his camera. "So who's this Lavinia woman?"

Travis took a breath. "Lavinia Major is the woman who stole one of your Aunt Norma's boyfriends away. She and Norma butted heads in a big way after that."

Griffin snorted. "I can imagine. I'm also surprised anyone could steal a man from Norma. Based on what I've heard, she wasn't the kind to let that happen. Or date a guy who would allow it."

"There's no definitive proof that Lavinia and Herb got together while he and Norma were still dating, but your aunt always believed that's what happened. So I don't know what the real story is, but as your aunt loved to point out, Lavinia was younger and apparently had looser morals."

Griffin snorted. "That could do it. This Herb guy, who was he?"

Maggie Miller

Travis frowned as he continued. "Herb Sorenson. Big local businessman. Herb was on the town council at the time and was instrumental in getting Norma the special allowance granted so she could build the inn's third story. Rumor is your aunt used her feminine charms to make that happen."

"Did she?"

Travis slanted his eyes at Griff. "I've been sworn to secrecy but let's just say rumor is a good word."

Griff nodded. "Got it."

"Norma really liked Herb. They were quite the item all throughout the building of the inn. He even officiated the ribbon cutting ceremony. But either around the time Norma and Herb broke it off or just before they broke it off, Norma found out that Herb was seeing Lavinia. Who also happened to be Norma's real estate agent."

"Ouch," Griffin said. "I can see how this escalated."

"Yep."

"Is Herb still alive?"

"No, he passed away a few years before Norma."

They walked up the driveway to the cottage's porch. "Did Norma retaliate against Lavinia?"

Travis nodded. "She did. She couldn't get out of the rental contract with her, so Norma let people stay rent free in the cottage for the remaining year that was left on the contract. When it expired, she took over the job of handling the rentals herself until she found out about those vacation rental websites, and then she moved it there."

Travis chuckled. "And Norma hated anything to do with computers, so that shows you how much animosity she had toward Lavinia."

Gulf Coast Secrets

"Apparently." Griffin opened the door. "Mom?"

She came out of the living room, Chloe in her arms, shaking her head. "This woman is taking her revenge on Norma through me, isn't she?"

Travis nodded. "Lavinia never could let go of a grudge."

Griffin held out the envelope. "This was delivered to the inn while we were there."

"Probably just a copy of the injunction," Travis said. "But I'm sure Roger will want it."

"He does," Georgia said. She didn't take the letter from Griffin. "Open it and see."

He did as she asked. "Yep, that's what it looks like."

"Okay. I need to get it to him. He's already working on a couple of things. A petition against the injunction as well as a claim of harassment against Lavinia for bringing up this charge."

Travis looked at the letter. "Can I see that?"

Griffin handed it over.

Travis skimmed it before looking up at them again. "My guess is your request for the new license triggered this. She's claiming that the special allowance for the third floor was only granted to Norma Merriweather and that the special allowance doesn't convey. In other words, it was granted to Norma and Norma alone. Anyone else is out of luck."

"That's ridiculous. What am I supposed to do? Chop off the third floor?"

Travis shook his head. "I don't see how this will stand, but it will delay things. I'm sure Lavinia knows that too. Not surprising she did this the day before the next town council meeting, either. She must be hoping to ram this through."

Maggie Miller

"There's a town council meeting tomorrow?" Georgia asked.

Travis nodded. "Seven p.m. at City Hall."

"Great." Georgia let out an enormous sigh. "We don't need any delays. Those cost money."

"Something else I'm sure Lavinia knows. And Diego and his crew are set to arrive any minute."

Griffin put his arm around his mom, who looked like she might cry. "We'll fix this. I'll run that letter over to Mr. Gillum's office for you."

"No, I can do it," Travis said. "Work on something else that doesn't involve being at the inn directly. There must be something you can do, right?"

Georgia took a breath. "I could get some of Norma's guest registries and start collecting names to send promotional postcards and invites to."

"I can go through my pictures," Griffin said. "Clean them up and get them ready to post. If we get to post them."

"You will," Travis said. "Keep working. I'll be back as soon as I can."

He headed out the door.

Griffin held out his hands to take Chloe. "I didn't know there was going to be drama."

Georgia gave the baby to him. "Me, either. I knew Norma had tangled with a few people, but I never anticipated we'd end up fighting those battles."

She put her hands on her hips. "You think I should text Mia? Let her know?"

Griffin gave Chloe his finger to grab onto. "No, let her finish her shift. She'll know soon enough."

Gulf Coast Secrets

His phone buzzed. He fished it out with one hand and checked the screen. "Hey, that's my new boss. Something's come up and she's got a job for me."

Georgia held her hands out to take Chloe back. "Go. None of us can afford to miss any income right now."

Maggie Miller

Gulf Coast Secrets

Chapter Fourteen

Mia looked up to greet her next customer in line and found herself face to face with Agatha Goodwin. "Hi, Agatha. How are you?"

There were no groceries on the conveyer belt and Agatha's sweet face held a very worried expression. "Mia, I need to talk to you right away."

"Is something wrong?" Mia asked.

"Yes," Agatha hissed in a conspiratorial whisper. "But we can't talk here."

Mia looked around for Lucas, to see if she could take a quick break. She had no idea what was going on, but Agatha looked distressed and Mia didn't want to leave the poor woman hanging. "Okay, just a second. Let me see if I can find a manager and take a break."

Lucas was a few aisles over, handling a void for another cashier.

"Lucas?" Mia called. "Can you come over here next?"

He looked over and smiled. "Be right there."

Maggie Miller

The woman behind Agatha looked perturbed.

Mia tipped her head toward the end of her lane. "Come stand over here, Agatha."

"Okay." She looked at the woman behind her, then glanced at the wine, ice cream and feminine products in her cart. "Sorry. You go on ahead."

Agatha moved out of the way while Mia got the other woman rung up and out the door.

Lucas came over. "Hey, Ms. Goodwin, how are you?"

Agatha clutched her purse in front of her. "I need to speak to Mia right away."

"Okay, sure." He gave Mia a nod. "Go ahead and take five."

"Thanks." Mia signed out of her register and stepped away so Lucas could take her place.

She walked with Agatha toward the front of the store. "What's going on? You seem upset."

"I am. That old biddy Lavinia is up to her tricks again."

Mia shook her head. "I don't know what that means."

"I just heard from Pearline, she's our bridge club alternate and she works at City Hall in the records department, that Lavinia has filed an injunction against all work being done at the inn. She's stopped you and your mom from doing anything, that old bag."

The words hit Mia like a cold bucket of water had been thrown on her. "What? Why would she do that?"

"I'm sure because she wants to get even with Norma, may she rest in peace." Agatha looked about ready to chew nails and Mia felt pretty much there herself.

"Because of the whole thing with Herb?"

Gulf Coast Secrets

Agatha nodded. "When your aunt rented out that cottage for free, Lavinia became the town laughingstock for a while. Norma bested her, no doubt about it. She never really lived it down."

"But Norma's dead. And that was ages ago. Why come after us?"

Agatha's steely eyes narrowed. "Because she can? Because she's a hateful old wench? Because...she's probably hoping you'll give up and sell the property."

"Like heck we will. Wow. I had no idea. I should call my mom."

"I'm sure she already knows. Word travels fast in this town."

"This is going to devastate her. She's already dealing with enough." Mia put her hand to her forehead. "I don't know what to do."

"We'll think of something," Agatha said. "The girls and me, I mean. We're not about to let Lavinia get away with this if we can help it. And we will definitely be at the town council meeting tomorrow. If for no other reason than moral support."

"There's going to be a town council meeting?"

Agatha nodded. "Yes. And I'm sure the timing is no coincidence. She did this the day before to try to push it through. Probably thinking you'd miss it or not show up because you're new and wouldn't understand the importance of showing up."

Mia blinked, a little dumbstruck by the whole thing. "I'm not sure we'd even have known."

Maggie Miller

"Well, like I said, we'll be there. If you or your mom has any questions, you call me."

"I will. Thanks. Let's stay in touch regardless. You have my number. If you come up with anything, let me know. And I'll do the same on my end."

Agatha nodded. "Good."

A familiar chime of three bells came over the PA system. "Good morning, Ludlow shoppers. Cranberry walnut bread is fresh out of the ovens in the bakery. Get yourself a loaf to take home while it's still warm."

Agatha's gaze shifted toward the bakery. "Oh, I love that bread. I'm going to get some." She put her hand on Mia's arm. "Listen, don't worry, honey. This isn't over yet. Not by a long shot."

Mia nodded and went back to her register, worried despite Agatha's reassurances. Stopping work would cost them time and time wasn't on their side when it came to the inn. Not when time was money and money was limited.

"You okay?" Lucas asked.

She shook her head slowly. "Someone's trying to stop my mom from opening the inn."

His brows bent. "Why would anyone do that?"

"An old grudge."

His brows reversed, shooting toward the sky. "That I can understand. There are some people in this town…" He just sighed. "Sorry. I shouldn't talk about our customers that way. But it's the truth. If you need anything, or there's anything I can do to help, just let me know."

"Thanks." She went back to work, pasting on a smile she didn't feel and keeping up the banter with everyone who came

Gulf Coast Secrets

through her line, but part of her brain was working away at the problem and how to solve it.

Unfortunately, she had no solution.

When her shift was finally over, she drove faster than she should have to get to the cottage. Her mom and Griffin's cars were in the driveway.

She raced inside. Both of them were working at the kitchen table. Griffin was on his laptop. Her mom had a pen and paper and a stack of the inn's guest registries, one open in front of her. Clyde was on the chair next to her mom, sleeping.

Mia greeted them as she came through the door. "Hey."

Georgia looked up. "Hi, honey. Not too loud, Chloe's sleeping."

"Finally," Griff said, glancing at his sister. "You're not going to believe what's going on."

"Yes, I am. Agatha from the thrift shop came into Ludlow's and told me all about Lavinia and her dirty tricks. Agatha's got the bridge club trying to figure out what to do. Their alternate, Pearline, works at City Hall."

Her mom looked pleasantly surprised. "Well, that's nice of them. Roger Gillum is working on it, too. He's already filed a counterclaim of harassment."

"Good. That's something at least." Mia took a seat. "I can't believe she'd do this. You know there's a town council meeting tomorrow night where this all gets decided?"

Georgia nodded. "Travis told us."

"Good. But man, we had better be prepared."

Griffin sat back in his chair. "I won't be as much help as I'd like. I got my first assignment today. I'm covering the meeting. I guess after I get my pictures I'll be free to join you, but until then I'm working."

"That's okay," Mia said. "In fact, I'm glad it's being documented." She squinted at a blank spot in front of her as her mind went into overdrive with a new idea. "Do you think your editor would be interested in doing an interview with mom? A community piece about the inn and keeping it in the family, bringing the business back to life for the good of local industry, that kind of thing?"

"Maybe. It's not a bad angle. I can call her."

Mia nodded. "Do that. Right now. We need to get ahead of this. And some good press would help. Fire with fire and all that."

Griffin grabbed his phone from next to his computer and started to dial. He walked to the back of the house. They could hear the sliders open and close as he went onto the deck.

Georgia grinned. "Mia Carpenter, I didn't know you could be so mercenary. It's kind of impressive."

Mia laughed. "I've never wanted anything so much as I want the chance to run this inn. I used to think the pinnacle of my life was to be married to Brenden and be a wife and have kids. Not anymore. I mean, sure, I still want to be married and have kids someday, but my immediate focus has completely changed. I want to make that inn the most successful inn this side of the Gulf Coast. I want to see it written up in travel magazines and loved on by social media influencers. I want our guests to have a better time than they thought possible. I want to earn the kinds of stars and reviews

Gulf Coast Secrets

on Yelp and Tripadvisor that make other inns ache with jealousy."

She leaned forward. "And I can't do any of that with Lavinia in our way."

Her mother's eyes went big. "Now I am definitely afraid of you." She laughed. "I'm glad you're on our side."

Griffin came back in. "Kelly said she'd love to do a piece. In fact, she can get it in the morning paper if we go over there right now."

"We?" Georgia said.

"Yep. Let's go," Griffin answered. "You and me."

"I can't go like this," Georgia said. "I need a few minutes to put myself together."

Griffin shook his head, smiling. "Well, hurry up, we're on a deadline."

"All right, all right." Georgia got up and went to her bedroom.

"Chloe will be fine with me," Mia said.

"Good, that was my next question. I got the pictures you asked for, although since Travis had to cancel the painters there wasn't as much rush."

Mia's mouth came open. "Oh no. That's not good. I didn't even think about that."

Griff shook his head. "Diego, the painter guy, said he had another job he could take for a day or two, but if the order isn't lifted soon, he might have to put us off for a few weeks."

A pit opened up in Mia's stomach. "That's worse than not good." She blew out a breath. "Griff, we can't let this happen."

"I know." He lowered his voice. "I worry what will happen to mom."

"Me, too. She's been so happy."

He glanced back toward the bedrooms, his jaw tight. "Then we just can't let it happen."

Gulf Coast Secrets

Chapter Fifteen

Travis knew what he was about to do might backfire, but then again, how much worse could things get? He parked outside of Lavinia Major's real estate office on Main Street and got out of his truck.

He stood there for a moment, getting his courage together and his anger under control. Staring up at her sign. Wishing she could have left well enough alone for once in her life.

But that wasn't Lavinia's way. Never had been.

The sign for her business, Major Real Estate also bore the slogan, *Every Sale is Major!* directly under the name.

That was Lavinia to a T. In fact, drama was probably her middle name. She thrived on it. And when there wasn't enough, she created some.

Like she was doing now. Like she'd done all those years ago.

He exhaled and walked through the front door.

Maggie Miller

The girl at the reception desk smiled at him. "Good morning. Welcome to Major Real Estate. How can we help you?"

"I need to speak to Lavinia, please."

"Do you have an appointment?"

"No, but I'm pretty sure she'll see me." She'd better, he thought.

"I believe she's got a showing. But I'd be happy to make an appointment for you. What time would be good for you?"

"*Now.*" Travis knew she was in her office. Her Mercedes was parked out front.

The girl picked up the phone. "Ms. Major, there's a man to see you."

She put the phone against her shoulder. "What did you say your name was?"

"Richie Rich. I want to buy the biggest house she has for sale." If that didn't do it, nothing would.

With a happily surprised look on her face, the girl put the phone back to her ear. "Mr. Rich is interested in our largest property. Yes, Ms. Major. Right away."

The girl put the phone back on its cradle, then stood. "Ms. Major will see you now. Would you like some coffee? Or a bottle of water?"

"No, I'm fine, thank you. I can see myself back." He went straight to Lavinia's office door and strode through.

She initially greeted him with a smile, but that disappeared the moment she made eye contact. "What are you doing here?"

He closed the door behind him. "I think you already know the answer to that question."

Gulf Coast Secrets

"I have nothing to say to you."

"That's fine. You can just listen." He planted himself in one of the chairs across from the pretentiously large desk.

"I will call the sheriff." Her hand inched toward the phone as if she might make good on her threat.

She wouldn't. He wasn't doing anything worth reporting. Yet. Not only that, but Grady would probably call her bluff. "Go ahead. Call the man I play poker with."

Frowning, she put her hand down. "What do you want?"

"Drop the injunction against the inn."

She barked out a laugh. "No. Unlike you, I care about the aesthetics of Blackbird Beach. That monstrosity never should have been built."

He just managed not to roll his eyes. "You don't care about aesthetics. If the zoning restrictions were changed tomorrow you'd be the first one in line to build a high rise. All you care about is you. Let's not play games."

She glared at him. "I'm not dropping the injunction. And there's nothing you can do about it."

He wasn't convinced of that. "Really? There's nothing I could offer you that would convince you otherwise?"

She blinked twice, like his offer had caught her off guard. "You care that much about the inn?"

He cared that much about Georgia. And her kids. And what this business was going to mean to them. But he wasn't about to tell Lavinia all that. She'd flip for sure. "It will bring a lot of much needed business to town. And it needs to be restored. For someone who claims to care about the aesthetics of our town, I'd think you'd want the inn to be rehabilitated. It looks abandoned right now."

"We could always just tear it down."

He sighed. "What do you want, Lavinia?"

She picked up a pen from her desk and tapped it against the arm of her chair as she sat back. "I could think of one thing."

"What?"

She smiled but there was nothing about her expression that made him happy. "You could leave town."

He stared at her. "You tried that before, remember?"

She nodded. "But this time, I'm taking a different approach. You leave town and I'll drop the injunction."

"Are you serious?"

Her slow nod told him she was. "Without you, what chance do they have of getting that place up and running? Especially when I can make sure no other contractor will work for them. Or for that matter, make sure their license isn't approved."

He couldn't take any more. He stood up. "You're a terrible excuse for a human being. I hope your life is as miserable as I think it is."

"You mean as miserable as yours?"

He'd already started for the door, but that made him stop and look at her again. "The only part of my life that's miserable is your doing. And if you take any joy or pride in that, then you aren't just a terrible person, you're also an evil one."

She huffed out a breath.

Anger surged up in him like a tsunami. "Do you believe in karma, Lavinia? Because if you do, you must be terrified of what's coming your way."

Gulf Coast Secrets

With that, he strode out before he did something there was no coming back from. The kind of thing he'd fantasized about over the years.

He got into his truck and turned the key to start the engine but didn't pull out of the parking spot. He needed a moment to calm down or he risked getting into an accident. Like with the Mercedes parked in front of him.

She was doing this to get at him. But Georgia and her family were the ones who'd take the hit. He couldn't let that happen. Which left him with two options.

He could leave town like Lavinia wanted.

Or he could come clean to Georgia.

Actually, he'd have to do both. He didn't see a way around it. Easy decision. He wasn't about to give Lavinia any joy. And if the inn went on, that would at least be a constant reminder of Norma's family doing well. As for him...he'd make a new life somewhere else. He could sell some of Cecil's sports memorabilia if necessary.

With a heavy heart, he drove straight back to the cottage.

But only Mia greeted him when he walked in. "Hey, Travis."

"Hey." He looked past her to see where Georgia was. "Is your mom here?"

"No, she and Griffin went into town. The Gazette is going to do a little feature on my mom and her plans to rehab and reopen the inn. They're going to publish it tomorrow so it'll be out before the town council meeting."

He wasn't sure that would help. "You mind if I get a cup of coffee and wait for them to get back?"

"No, help yourself."

Maggie Miller

He went to the pot and poured himself a cup.

"Everything all right? You seem…not yourself," Mia said.

Was it that obvious? He turned and leaned on the counter. He didn't want to tell his story twice, but he wasn't sure he could keep it in. "I need to talk to your mom."

Maybe he shouldn't stay. He could come back after all. He only lived a short distance away.

He stared into his coffee, wondering how Georgia would react. Fire him? It was certainly within her right. And to be honest, it would be a smart thing to do. To distance herself from him. But he wasn't going down that easily. He'd explain his plan to fight. To have his say at last. And pray she understood.

But standing there, doing nothing, made the waiting unbearable. He put his cup on the counter. "I'm going over to the inn to finish painting the kitchen."

She frowned. "I thought we couldn't work over there because of the injunction."

"We can't, but how is anyone going to know I'm in there? And if someone actually comes by to check, I'll just say I'm cleaning up. We can't leave it unfinished like that."

She smiled. "Okay. Thanks."

He nodded but didn't have it in him to smile back. "Text me when your mom returns?"

"Will do."

He took one more sip of his coffee, then headed to the inn. He left his truck parked on the curb outside of Georgia's cottage. Moving it to the inn would only attract attention, and he firmly believed that Lavinia would send someone to check. But he'd take the risk. *And* the blame if it came to that.

Gulf Coast Secrets

Finishing the kitchen was the least he could do. He went inside but didn't turn on any lights. There was no point in attracting unnecessary attention.

He'd just about finished when his phone buzzed with a message. He figured it was Mia telling him Georgia was home, so he put off looking at the text for a few more minutes. He touched up the last few spots, then stood back to check his work. Happy with how it looked, he nodded. The kitchen was done.

He might be too, but he felt better about having accomplished this much.

He took his phone out and checked the screen. It was from Mia, as expected.

Mom and Griff just got back.

Heading over, he replied.

On his way out, he stopped in the foyer and took one last look around. He loved this place. And he'd absolutely loved the woman who'd owned it and made him feel like he was part of her family.

"Sorry, Norma. But this is the best way I know how to protect them."

He went through the door, closing it behind him and feeling very much like it was for the last time.

Maggie Miller

Gulf Coast Secrets

Chapter Sixteen

Georgia felt good about the interview. Kelly Singh had been very kind and her questions had seemed not only fair but asked with genuine interest and good will. Now Georgia just hoped that enough people read the interview to understand what she wanted to do.

And that those people sympathized with her. She needed people on her side.

Mia was still working at the kitchen table. She looked up from her phone. "Hey guys. Travis is coming over. He wants to talk to you, Mom. He was here earlier but decided to go work at the inn until you got home."

Georgia shook her head. "What about the injunction?"

"Hah," Griffin shook his head. "Travis isn't about to let that stop him. Have you met that guy?"

"Yeah." Mia nodded. "He said he'd keep it on the downlow."

Georgia slanted her eyes at her daughter. "I doubt very much Travis said on the downlow."

Mia snorted. "I was paraphrasing. How was the interview?"

"You two discuss," Griffin said. "I'm going to check on Chloe."

"It was good," Georgia answered. "She asked about my motivation for restoring and reopening the inn, how it was going, what I was looking forward to most, how I liked Blackbird Beach, that kind of stuff."

"Cool. Sounds a little like a fluff piece, but that's totally okay. Fluff is good. Did you get to talk about the community side of things?"

"I did." Georgia nodded. "I told her we very much want to be a part of the community and how you'd already extended the invite to the local bridge club to start meeting at the inn again."

"Awesome." Mia smiled. "Of course, you have to abide by that now. But Agatha will love it. Oh! That reminds me. I should tell her about the interview. We're keeping each other in the loop."

Through the front windows, Georgia spied Travis coming up the walk. She opened the door. "Hey there. I heard you were being sneaky."

He frowned as he climbed the porch steps. "What?"

She moved out of the way so he could come in. "Mia said you went over to do some painting despite the injunction."

"Oh, that. Yeah. I figured I could at least get the kitchen finished. And I did."

"Thank you." Georgia's intuition kicked in. Although it didn't take much to see he wasn't himself. He seemed down. "What's going on? You wanted to talk to me?"

Gulf Coast Secrets

He nodded. "All of you, I guess. Is Griffin here?"

Griffin came out of the bedroom, holding Chloe. "I'm here."

Travis took a breath. "I need to tell you all something. This injunction is my fault."

Griffin snorted. "I highly doubt that."

"No, it is." Travis took his ballcap off and raked a hand through his hair. "Lavinia isn't doing this to you all so much as she's doing it to me. She and I have butted heads for a long time. Not just because of Norma either."

"But why?" Georgia asked. "That makes no sense. What could she have against you?"

He swallowed, the muscles in his jaw tightening. "A lot. Lavinia Major is my ex-mother-in-law."

Georgia stared at him, momentarily at a loss for words.

He shook his head, staring at a spot on the floor in front of him. "I never anticipated she'd come after you to get to me. But it certainly feels like that's what she's doing now. And I apologize. I know what a terrible spot I've put you in. I'm sorry for that too."

When she didn't say anything, he exhaled and kept talking. "I'll have my stuff cleaned out of the cottage as soon as I can, but I will still be going to the council meeting. You may not like me being there, but I'm going to have my say before I leave."

"You're leaving? Why are you leaving? You can't leave." Georgia gaped at him, trying to make sense of it all.

He lifted his head. "Because I caused all this trouble. Don't you want me gone?"

Maggie Miller

Her mouth fell open. "No. Not even a tiny bit. We need you, Travis."

Mia and Griffin nodded, but neither said a word.

Travis didn't look convinced. "But I caused this."

"No, you didn't." She was using her sternest mom voice now, but she couldn't stop herself. It just came out when she was this level of frustrated. "Are you nuts? Lavinia caused this."

"Georgia, she's doing this because of me. She blames me for her daughter moving away and taking her grandchild and great grandchild."

"Why didn't Lavinia move with Jillian and Sam then? She could have gone."

"Too stubborn. Too entrenched in business here. And I believe part of her thought Jillian was bluffing. That it was her daughter's ploy to get me to come crawling after her. When I didn't…I went to the top of Lavinia's hit list."

"Was that why she took up with Herb? To punish Norma for your imagined sins?"

"I'm sure that entered into it but she always blamed Cecil for stealing that land away from her. Not that Lavinia had the money to afford it. No one in Blackbird Beach did. It wasn't cheap. That's why it sat so long."

Mia stood up. She looked stricken. And a little panicky. "Please don't leave, Travis. My mom's right. We really do need you. I don't care what Lavinia tries, we'll find a way around her."

"You won't. She owns that town council. They'll do what she says." He frowned. "Her ultimate goal is to buy the inn and tear it down. She says it's ruining the aesthetics of

Gulf Coast Secrets

Blackbird Beach, but she wants to own that property more than anything."

New resolve stiffened Georgia's spine. "She will never have that inn or that land. Not over my dead body. Norma wouldn't give in, would she?"

For the first time since he'd entered the cottage, Travis smiled. "No, she wouldn't."

Georgia's phone rang. Roger Gillum. She answered quickly. "This is Georgia."

"Ms. Carpenter, I have disappointing news. I've read through the injunction as well as the original council allowance and the agreement that Norma signed. Unfortunately, it's binding. Had I been her attorney at the time, I never would have let her sign that. I wasn't, however, and she did."

Georgia had to swallow before she could speak. "What do we do now?"

"You'll have to request a new allowance from the council. This time in perpetuity. We can continue with the counterclaim of course, but I'm not sure we have much standing should this go before a judge."

"Okay. Thank you."

"Rest assured I will continue to investigate this issue. If I find anything, I'll let you know immediately."

"Thanks." She hung up, taking a moment to process. "Roger Gillum says the allowance really was written only to apply to Norma's ownership of the inn. We don't just need to get the council to drop the injunction. We need them to grant us a new allowance."

Maggie Miller

They all went silent for a moment as the weight of that settled over them. Georgia felt defeated, but then she thought about her aunt and what she would do. Norma wouldn't give up this easily.

So neither would she. "All right, we need a new plan." Georgia looked at Mia. "Call Agatha, see if she's found out anything. Or if she has any ideas about how we can combat Lavinia. You said there was a whole bridge club that were friends of Norma's? Get them involved too. In fact, go see Agatha. Talk to her in person and take notes."

Mia nodded. "I'm on it. They'll help. Agatha already said she'd bring the girls to the council meeting for moral support."

"Good. We're going to need it." Then Georgia turned to Griffin. "You need to go back to the Gazette and talk to Kelly. Tell her what Lavinia's planning. Ask her if she knows anything about Lavinia that might help us."

Griffin hitched Chloe a little higher up on his shoulder. "Are you going to stay here and watch Chloe?"

Georgia shook her head. "I'm going to stay here, but you're taking Chloe with you. I doubt very highly that a young woman like Kelly couldn't be softened up by the presence of that sweet little baby."

Griffins brows shot up. "Are you suggesting I use my daughter's charms to get Kelly on our side?"

Georgia grinned. "This is war. Everything and everyone are fair game."

"Wow, Mom," he answered, clearly a little amused. "I've never seen you like this."

Gulf Coast Secrets

"You can blame your father. After the way he's treated me, I'm done being a pushover." She pulled out her phone and dialed Roger Gillum. As it rang, she snapped her fingers to get her kids' attention. "Let's go. The clock's ticking."

Mia and Griffin jumped, grabbing their keys and preparing to leave.

Travis chuckled softly. "You are something else. What can I do?"

Georgia was about to answer him when Mr. Gillum's receptionist, Flora, answered. "Good afternoon, Roger Gillum's office."

"Flora, this is Georgia Carpenter. How are things going with the injunction? I was hoping for an update."

"The counterclaim has been filed, but that's about it so far. Do you want to speak to him?"

"Just give him a message. We're fighting this as hard as we can. If there's anything else he can think of for us to do or to have him do, I want to know about it."

"Will do. You have a good day."

"You too." Georgia hung up.

Mia had already left and Griffin was on his way out, Chloe in her car seat carrier, her diaper bag slung over his shoulder.

"That was impressive," Travis said. "Now, what can I do?"

"You and I are going digging."

He made a face. "Digging? For what?"

"Dirt." She grinned. "Come on." She grabbed her purse and her keys and walked out of the cottage.

He followed. "You're not telling me where we're going?"

"To the inn."

His eyes narrowed. "To do what?"

Maggie Miller

"I have a hunch. That's all." She pulled the door shut and locked it, then started down the walk at a far clip.

He kept up. "You think Norma has something to tell you?"

"I think she might have something to help us, that's all." She gave him a sly smile. "She knew all about Lavinia. And your history with her. She got back at Lavinia for Herb a little bit by renting out the cottage free for a year, but I just have a feeling that wasn't enough."

"I don't know."

"I do. She loved you. And she knew Lavinia had it in for you. Norma would have wanted insurance. A way to slap Lavinia back if the time came. And well, the time has come. We just have to figure out what that insurance was."

His brows rose. "You might be on to something there."

She went through the gate and jogged up the steps to the inn, taking her keys out as she went. "We're about to find out."

Gulf Coast Secrets

Chapter Seventeen

Travis hadn't expected to return to the inn ever, let alone this soon, but Georgia's willingness to keep him around was a sharp reminder that she wasn't a woman he should ever underestimate.

She was also very much Norma's relative. And for that, he would be eternally grateful. "How do you want to do this?"

"Divide and conquer," she said. "You're in charge of the attic while I'll handle her little office under the stairs."

"And we're looking for?"

"Anything that could be considered dirt on Lavinia. Newspaper clippings, legal paperwork, photographs, diary entries…I don't know for sure but it'll be clear, I hope, when we find it. But I suspect we're going to have to look pretty thoroughly. Norma wouldn't leave something like that just laying around."

"Okay. And I agree, but I have to say, the thought of digging through Norma's personal things gives me some weird feelings. She was such a private person."

"I know. I feel that way too. But I feel confident she wouldn't mind us doing this one bit. Considering the cause and all."

"Agreed." There was no one Norma had liked less than Lavinia. He started for the steps but as he hit the first one, he paused and looked over his shoulder. "I'll text you if I find anything."

"Okay, me too." She smiled. "I'm sorry you thought for one second that I wouldn't stand by you because of Lavinia. If I've had anything reinforced in my short time here, it's that family matters first and foremost. And you were family to Norma."

He couldn't help but ask the question that popped into his head. "So I'm...family to you?"

Her smile widened. "I don't want to say that because it would be weird to kiss family the way I want to kiss you."

Caught off-guard by her comment, he belly-laughed. "Well then. Good to know."

She was blushing, but still smiling as she looked toward the back of the house. "And on that note, I'm going to work."

"Me, too." He practically ran up the two flights of steps. She considered him like family. But she wanted to kiss him again. He wanted to kiss her too again. When she was ready.

The idea was enough to lighten his mood considerably. He opened the attic door and flipped on the light.

And was immediately struck by the job that lay ahead of him. There was so much to go through that the only reasonable way to do it was to start at one side and work his way around.

Gulf Coast Secrets

He wasn't sure he could do it all in a week, let alone the time they had before the council meeting. But he was going to try. He'd stay here until the council meeting, if that's what it took. Lavinia had cowed people in Blackbird Beach for too long.

It was time for a reckoning.

He started with the left-hand side closest to the door. The first thing was an old dresser with boxes stacked on top. He took the boxes down, surprised at how heavy they were, and set them on the floor, then systematically went through the drawers, checking the interior of each one as well as feeling underneath to make sure there wasn't anything hidden there.

But the dresser had no secrets to share.

The boxes were next. He pulled out his pocketknife and split the tape on the first one. Books. Old books. He took them all out, leafed through each one and even gave them a shake. Nothing.

After he repacked them and put the box on the dresser again, he started on the second box. More books. He treated them the same way as the others and found the same thing. Nothing.

As frustrating as it was, he kept going.

But none of the boxes that had come off the dresser bore any fruit. He started on the next thing, a desk. It had numerous drawers and compartments and he spent at least ten minutes looking through all of them.

He found an old Chinese take-out menu, a rubber band, and half of a broken pencil, none of which held any promise.

Maggie Miller

With a sigh, he moved on, wondering if Georgia was having the same kind of luck he was. He hoped not. But then his phone hadn't gone off either.

This was going to take forever.

* * *

Georgia stood looking into Norma's cubbyhole office for a moment, trying to decide where to look first. Her office was tucked under the stairs in a sort of secret compartment and though it was small, it was stuffed to the gills with books, paperwork, mementos, and knickknacks.

Georgia had never really thought of Norma as a hoarder, and she still didn't, but it was clear her aunt had surrounded herself with her favorite things. The corkboard that covered half of one sidewall held all sorts of things, from a single dried rose to a baggie of sand. More papers, too. Many with Norma's handwritten notes on them.

But at the center was a framed wedding photo of Norma and Cecil. Never far from where she could see it. Georgia peered closer and realized the wedding dress Norma had on looked very much like the one in the box she'd found.

That made Georgia smile for a moment. Then she straightened and focused on all the other things in the office that she was now going to have to sort through with a keen eye. So much stuff.

The two filing cabinet drawers seemed the most likely place to store the kind of information she was looking for. But did that kind of obviousness make them the least likely?

Trying to think like her aunt was impossible. The woman's mind had been something special and it was a rare occasion that she wasn't two or three steps—or more—ahead of the average person.

Which was more reason to think that she'd prepared for this eventuality. Norma had to have known Lavinia wasn't about to stop holding her grudges.

Georgia sighed. She was wasting time. The filing cabinet was as good a place to start as any.

She sat in the desk chair, turned it toward the cabinet, and opened the first drawer, slightly surprised to see it actually held hanging files. She'd expected a stack of papers, but then Norma had run a successful business. She hadn't managed that by not being organized.

The files were organized by company name or a general header, like Linens. Or Garden Ideas. Or Frank's Aluminum.

An interesting mix for sure, but sadly there was no Lavinia Major category. Nor was there a file labeled Archrivals or Annoying People or Disreputable Realtors. Georgia smiled. She wouldn't have been surprised to see any of those, truth be told.

Even so, she carefully looked through each file to be sure she wasn't missing something that might have a double meaning.

The one marked Future Plans looked promising. But that was really all it held. Interestingly enough, there were plans inside for a gazebo in the back, something Georgia had been thinking about herself. She held that file out for more consideration.

She kept going through each one, checking the headers and opening the file of any that sounded interesting. But

Maggie Miller

when she reached the back of the drawer, she still had nothing about Lavinia.

She opened the second drawer and found more of the same hanging files. These however seemed more personal in nature, the headers were things like Taxes, Marriages, Recipes, Family Birthdays.

Georgia's interest instantly picked up. This could be the right drawer. After all, wasn't Lavinia a more personal matter? Georgia certainly thought so.

It also felt like she was looking into who Norma was. Georgia had no idea that her aunt had kept a file on birthdays. Just out of curiosity she pulled that folder and had a look.

It was just a couple sheets of paper with the names of all her family members on it. Next to each name were a few scribbled notes.

Next to Mia's name was written *likes horses, purple and Nancy Drew books.*

Georgia smiled. That had definitely been true of Mia when she was a little girl. And she still liked purple.

Next to Georgia's name was scrawled a few more things. *Likes baking, good cook, deserves better.*

Georgia stared at those last two words. She felt a pang of something she couldn't quite name. Maybe it was Norma's care for her, or maybe it was Norma's ability to recognize what Georgia hadn't even known about herself then. She did deserve better and Norma, in her own way, had made sure Georgia got it.

Deserves better.

And now she had it.

Gulf Coast Secrets

Those two words made Georgia surprisingly weepy. She wiped her eyes. There wasn't time to dwell on this right now, but those two words weren't something she was soon going to forget.

She went back to looking through the folders. Going through the one marked Marriages would have probably led her down some interesting paths, but again Georgia didn't have the time. She went back to searching for anything to do with Lavinia but just like with the first drawer she reached the end and had found nothing.

She sighed and took another long, hard look at the small space. The desk was stacked with paperwork, envelopes, notebooks, flyers…all kinds of things. Then there was the shelf of ledgers. Travis had told them Norma had kept a daily record in them of the weather, how many guests were at the inn, and maybe a note or two about what the day's activities were.

Again, Georgia could have gotten lost in those, but that didn't seem like a place Norma would have put anything about Lavinia. Those were all about the inn.

Above that shelf was a row of cubbyholes. They were all filled. Some of them held knickknacks, decorative little boxes, more papers, tickets to shows, plays, and concerts Norma had gone to, invites, notices, all kinds of things.

The amount of stuff seemed endless.

Georgia decided to tackle the cubbyholes next. She cleared a little space on the desk and took out everything from the first one.

Lots of interesting things but nothing that seemed related to Lavinia. She went through each one with the same care. In the third one, there was a small lidded ceramic box. She took it down and opened it and found a gorgeous amethyst, pearl, and diamond ring.

It looked real to Georgia, but she was no expert on fine jewelry. She glanced up the cubbyholes again. The last one had a little carved wooden box in it. She took it down, opened it up and found more jewelry.

This time an emerald and diamond pendant.

Georgia shook her head. If Norma had such valuable things tucked away like this, there was no telling where she might have put information on Lavinia.

All they could do was look. And hope.

Gulf Coast Secrets

Chapter Eighteen

She finished the office and still hadn't come across anything. She rubbed her forehead. Had she missed anything? Or had she been wrong? Maybe she had been. But her gut still believed Norma had something for her to find.

Something that would help her win against Lavinia.

Georgia leaned back in the chair, tipping her head up as she exhaled in frustration.

Which was when she noticed a keyhole in the ceiling.

Odd place for a keyhole. She got up to examine it better. Looked like a little door, actually, set lengthwise in the ceiling. She opened the top drawer of the desk where she'd seen a hairpin and got it out. She stuck one end in the lock and fiddled around, trying to open the mysterious hidey-hole.

The hairpin didn't do anything except make a little noise.

She tossed it back onto the desk and stared up at the keyhole. It was no wonder she hadn't noticed it before. For one thing, she hadn't really spent any time in this room. Mia had been the one to gather the guest registries. But if she'd

Maggie Miller

noticed the latch over her head, she hadn't said anything about it.

For another the keyhole's metal surround was painted white to match the ceiling.

The key to the office was on her keyring. She fished it out of her purse, separated it from the others, and tried it.

Didn't work. Which was extremely frustrating because now she had to go back to the cottage and get the tangle of keys Roger Gillum had originally given her.

The key had to be on that ring, because Aunt Norma wouldn't have a little hiding spot like this and not leave Georgia the key.

Would she?

She texted Travis. *Found a locked hiding spot but need a key. Going back to the cottage for key ring.*

She didn't wait for him to answer, just tucked her phone away and headed for the front door.

He yelled down from the landing before she made it out. "Georgia."

She stopped and look up at him. "Do you have a key?"

"No, but I could try to pick it."

"I already did that with a hair pin. No luck."

"Yes, but I have the feeling you didn't have the misspent youth I did." He smiled. "Just saying I might be better at picking locks than you are."

She laughed. "You're probably right. Okay, sure, if you want to try."

He jogged down the steps, reaching her a few moments later. "Where did you find this hiding spot?"

"In her office."

Gulf Coast Secrets

Travis frowned. "I don't remember any hiding spots in there. Not that I spent any real time in there. That was strictly your aunt's domain. And I guess it wouldn't have been much of a hiding spot if I knew about it."

"Good point." She took him into the office and pointed at the ceiling. "Right there."

He stared up at the keyhole. "How about that? All these years, I never knew that was there."

"So? Do you think you can pick it?"

"I can sure give it a try." He reached into his pocket and took out a Swiss army style pocketknife. His had a wooden shell as opposed to a red one. He opened up one of the many arms to a long, slim tool with a little hooked end. It almost looked like a crochet hook, but Georgia knew better. He held out his other hand. "Give me that hairpin too, please."

She picked it up off the desk and put it in his hand. Then she watched closely, hoping she might learn something. Being able to pick a lock seemed like a very useful life skill to have.

He bent the hairpin and then took one side of it and the tool from his knife and inserted them both into the lock and began to work on it, pressing with one and poking with the other.

Seconds ticked by and nothing seemed to happen. Nothing did happen. He didn't quit. But then after another minute, he shook his head. "This isn't going so well. Just like your aunt to have a lock that I can't pick."

A few more seconds and he finally gave up, making a noise that sounded like a cross between a growl and a groan. "We'll have to find the key."

Maggie Miller

She nodded. "I'm off to the cottage to grab the set I got from Mr. Gillum. I'm sure it's on there. That key ring has a ton of keys."

"All right," he said. He tossed the hairpin onto the desk and put his knife in his pocket. "I'm going to head back up to the attic and keep looking. There is every possibility that there is nothing in this little cabinet. Although…there might be a safe in there."

"Really?"

He nodded. "I always thought she had one. Somewhere. You didn't find one in the bedroom?"

"I didn't. And if Mia did, she didn't say anything about it." She sighed. "Norma sure liked to hide things away, didn't she?"

"She liked her mysteries, that's for sure."

"Look at what I found earlier." Georgia picked up the two small boxes she had discovered in the cubbyholes. "I'm pretty sure the jewelry inside these is real."

She opened the boxes to show him.

He nodded. "Those are definitely real. Both were gifts from Cecil. I know because she used to wear them a lot and she would tell me that he had given them to her. The amethyst ring was a pre-engagement present. The emerald I think was bought on their cruise."

Good to know they were the genuine article. "Why would she keep them in here?"

He shrugged. "Maybe because those were two of her favorite pieces and she liked to have them close? Norma's decisions didn't always make sense to anyone but her."

Gulf Coast Secrets

Georgia closed up the boxes and put them back in their original spots. "I could see keeping meaningful pieces nearby."

"She definitely held onto things that meant something to her."

Georgia ran her fingers over the framed wedding picture. "She never stopped missing him, did she?"

Travis shook his head. "Not for a single day."

Georgia stared at the photo for a second longer. Then she looked at Travis. "I'll go get the keys."

He nodded. "I'll be in the attic if you need me."

They both left the office behind and walked to the foyer. From there, he veered off and went up the steps and she went out the door. As she left the inn, she noticed a car pulling away from the curb. Had Lavinia sent someone to check up on them?

Georgia stared after the car, anger bubbling up inside her. What was wrong with that woman that she had nothing else going on in her life but to bother a family trying to make a new start? Who was that petty?

Okay, maybe Lavinia was mad at Travis for family reasons. But that was no excuse for Lavinia to destroy the life Georgia was trying to make here.

She shook her head and walked to her cottage, trying to calm herself down. Being angry wasn't going to help. She went into her bedroom and grabbed the big ring of keys from the top drawer of her nightstand.

As she walked back to the inn, she looked through the keys to find one that seemed about the size of the lock. There were three to pick from. And no way of knowing which one might work without trying them.

Back inside she went straight to the office with the keys in hand. The first key fit into the lock but wouldn't turn. The second key was too big. The third key was too small, wiggling around with no purchase. She sighed in frustration. She felt like Goldilocks without the key that was just right.

Should she call a locksmith? Maybe. Or maybe she should call her kids and ask them what to do? Or see if they had any ideas?

She thought about that for a moment. Was there any chance that Norma had given her friends from the bridge club any clues that might help Georgia find what she needed to about Lavinia? Mia was with them now.

Georgia took out her phone and called. This was too much of a conversation to have via text.

Mia answered right away. "Hey, Mom. Any luck?"

"Yes and no. But first, listen. Has Agatha or any of her friends said anything about what possible insurance Norma might have against Lavinia?"

"I asked and nothing yet, but they're talking amongst themselves trying to figure out what it might be. Now, back up. What do you mean yes and no?"

"I mean we're looking but we haven't uncovered anything yet."

"That sounds like just a no. What's the yes part?"

Georgia shook her head as if Mia could see her. "I found a locked panel in the ceiling of Norma's office under the stairs, but none of the keys on my key ring will open it and Travis couldn't pick it so it's a no."

Gulf Coast Secrets

"What about the key you found?"

Georgia squinted as her heart skipped a beat. "What key?"

"Remember? In that beautiful Chanel tote I found in Aunt Norma's closet?"

Georgia sucked in a breath as the memory came back. "It completely slipped my mind. How could I forget that? Yes. What did we do with that key? You took it, right?" That part she didn't remember.

"No, you held onto it. I think you were going to hang it on the hook inside Aunt Norma's closet. Go get it, then try it and call me right back. I'll see what the girls can tell me in the meantime."

Georgia smiled at Mia calling Agatha and her senior citizen friends girls. It was very cute. "Good, thanks, will do."

She hung up and went right to the closet. The key was exactly where Mia had said, hanging on the hook by the black silk ribbon looped through the top of it.

She took it down and turned it over in her fingers. The scrollwork top was shinier than the rest of it. Could that really be it? Only one way to tell.

Straight back to the office and she put the key in the lock. It fit perfectly. She held her breath as she turned it, expecting to meet resistance.

But she didn't.

Maggie Miller

Gulf Coast Secrets

Chapter Nineteen

Diaper bag over one shoulder, car seat carrier in the other hand, Griffin pushed through the door of the Blackbird Gazette's office. "Kelly?"

She was at her desk, where she almost always was. She looked up, smiling as she took her glasses off and stuck them on top of her head. He'd wondered more than once if she kept her hair in that messy bun to keep her glasses from falling back. "Hi, Griffin. What can I do for you?"

He walked in, about to answer, when her gaze went straight to Chloe.

Kelly let out a little gasp as she smiled and leaned forward to see better. "Is that your daughter?" She laughed. "Silly question. What other baby would you be carrying? Oh, she's beautiful."

She wiggled her fingers at Chloe. "Hi, peanut."

He smiled. His mother had been right. "Thanks." He looked down at his child. "Chloe, this is my boss, Kelly Singh."

Kelly got up and came around to crouch in front of the carrier. "Hello there, Miss Chloe. Aren't you just the prettiest thing? Yes you are."

Kelly stood, her eyes still on Chloe. "What a doll. You and your wife must be so happy."

"I'm not married."

She looked at him. "You're not? I didn't notice a ring but then a lot of men don't wear them. Are you divorced then?" She shook her head. "Sorry, reporter habit of asking too many questions."

"No, it's okay. Not divorced either. To be perfectly frank, Chloe's mother dropped her off on my doorstep two weeks ago and that was how I found out I had a daughter."

"Wow." Kelly stared at him, her brows arching. "Are you serious? That's crazy. Who does that?"

He shrugged. "I guess she couldn't handle being a mom. It's definitely hard work taking care of a baby."

Chloe gurgled, kicking her feet.

"You seem to be doing all right."

"Thanks, but she's the reason I moved here. To be close to my mom and sister and honestly, get some help with Chloe.

Kelly looked at her again. "But to give up a child…at least she gave her over to you. That's something to be thankful for."

"I am, believe me," Griffin said. "Taking care of her is a full-time job, but it's also the most rewarding thing I've ever done."

"I bet." Kelly sighed, a sound that had a hint of longing in it. Then she raised her eyes to Griffin again. "I guess we got

Gulf Coast Secrets

a little off topic there. Unless you came in to introduce Chloe to me?"

"No, I came in because I need some help. That is, my family needs some help. Do you have a couple minutes?"

She nodded. "Sure. What's going on?"

"Do you know who Lavinia Major is?"

Kelly barked out a sharp laugh. "Everyone in this town knows who Lavinia Major is." Then she schooled her face into a more neutral expression. "Sorry, that was unprofessional of me. Yes, I am aware of her. May I ask why?"

"She's filed an injunction against the inn to stop all work from being done. She's claiming the third floor was given to my great Aunt Norma by special license and that license does not extend to the next owner, who just happens to be my mother."

Kelly's mouth came open and her eyes lit up like a switch had been flipped inside her. "She's a piece of work, that one."

She put her hands on her hips. "In the interest of full disclosure, my dad owns this paper. He bought it when it was about to go out of business and gave it to me to run. I was a journalism major and there weren't a lot of papers hiring, but he also wanted to preserve this one. I know that sounds like I didn't earn my way into this job, which in all fairness, I didn't, but I made the paper profitable in its second year so I am definitely earning my pay now. Anyway, I'm telling you that because it's backstory and it's relevant."

He nodded, not sure he fully understood just yet.

She went on. "When I initially took over as editor, one of the first people to stop by and congratulate me was Lavinia.

Maggie Miller

She brought me a plant and wished me well and immediately signed up for a half page of advertising in every Friday paper. I was grateful, to say the least. Ads are how we keep the doors open. I was so encouraged by what I thought was her kind outreach to the Gazette."

"It wasn't?"

She frowned. "Not exactly. Do you know that a few days after I sent all the advertising bills out, she had the nerve to march back in here with the bill and explain to me that she didn't pay for ads because without her, no one else would advertise? That she was helping me by setting an example for other business owners in town?"

Kelly's face had turned the slightest shade of indignant plum. "I mean, the nerve. Would she be okay if I asked her to list a property for me and then not take a commission on it when it sold?"

"I have a feeling she wouldn't be."

"Not even for a minute."

"So what did you do?"

Her eyes narrowed but that did nothing to diminish the fire in them. "It pains me to say this, but I had to let it slide."

"Really?" That shocked him. Kelly didn't seem like the kind of woman who'd back down so easily.

She nodded, clearly frustrated. "At first I told her the bill had to be paid. Within a day, I had a handful of other advertisers who'd called to cancel their ads. I couldn't believe it."

"She has that much power?"

"She does. To make matters worse, she's up for reelection next month and will once again run uncontested and be right

Gulf Coast Secrets

back in the seat of power she uses to control this town." She pursed her lips and blew out a breath like she was trying to get rid of her frustrations along with it. "Lavinia Major is the cost of doing business in Blackbird Beach."

A wild, crazy idea formed in Griffin's mind. Possibly from lack of sleep thanks to Chloe, but he might have also just been emboldened by such an imbalance of power in his new town. "What if she didn't run uncontested?"

Kelly stared at him like he hadn't heard a word she'd just said. "No one will run against her. They're all scared of her."

He shook his head. "Not all of us. Here's what I'm proposing. You help us find enough leverage to defeat Lavinia at the town council meeting tomorrow night and I'll run against her. If we win, that is. If we don't…I'm not sure we'll be able to stay in town."

She continued to stare at him. "You're serious."

"Why not? I'm old enough to be a councilman, aren't I?"

"You only have to be eighteen according to the town bylaws."

"And I'm twenty-seven. Is there a residency restriction?"

She bit her bottom lip, then turned around and went to her desk, putting her glasses back on. She started tapping away at her keyboard and a few seconds later, answered him. "You have to have a Blackbird Beach address at which you reside."

But then she closed her eyes briefly, opening them to shake her head as she stared at her computer screen. "And you have to have lived there at least a year."

His mood sank. "So much for that. I mean, I could definitely run in a year's time. But that doesn't do us any good right now."

"And you couldn't do it for two years, actually. That's how long the terms run."

He sighed. "Would your dad do it?"

"No. He's already too busy and if he takes on another thing, my mom will kill him. Figuratively, of course." She tipped her head down so she could look over her lens at him. "Do you know anyone you could convince to run?"

He thought for a second. There were two people who immediately came to mind. One was Roger Gillum, but the man already had his hands full of work for them. Griffin couldn't imagine he'd be willing to add councilman to his plate. Even if it was for a worthy cause.

The other person that came to mind was Travis. But would he? Maybe. He certainly had no love for Lavinia. But would that be enough? Considering his history with Aunt Norma, it just might be. "Possibly. I'd have to talk to him first."

"Of course. If it helps, tell him I'll put the full force of the Gazette behind him. I'll even have the paper endorse him and we've never endorsed a candidate yet."

"Yeah?"

She nodded. "I promise."

He smiled. "Okay. Then we have work to do. We need as many reasons as possible for the council to permit that third-floor allowance to carry over to my mom."

"It's not going to be easy." She pushed her glasses a little higher on the bridge of her nose. "But I love a challenge. Let's get to it."

Gulf Coast Secrets

Chapter Twenty

As soon as Georgia realized the key was going to unlock the panel, she stopped. Travis should be here. This was as much about him as it was about her and the inn. Both of their futures depended on this.

Which suddenly felt like a lot of pressure.

She took out her phone and texted him. *Found the key. Come downstairs.*

She hit send, then walked out of the office to wait for him. She paced in the hall, but it didn't take long for him to respond. It wasn't by text either. She immediately heard footsteps thundering down the stairs above.

He called out as he turned on the landing. "What was in there? Did you find anything you could use?"

"I haven't opened it yet. I wanted to wait for you."

He came around into the hall, smiling. "You waited for me?"

Maggie Miller

She lifted one shoulder. "Seemed like a moment you should share. It affects both of us. Although I just realized I may have called you down here for nothing. It could be empty."

"Like Al Capone's vault?" He laughed. "Your aunt didn't have a secret locked hiding spot just to keep it empty."

"I hope you're right. We'll see in just a second."

He followed her back into the tiny office.

They both stared up at the ceiling. She put her hand on the key, which she'd left sticking out of the lock, and turned.

A little click and the panel was unlocked.

She looked at Travis.

"Fingers crossed," he said.

She opened the panel. It unhinged like a door hanging down from the ceiling. Through the opening she could see the underside of the stair treads. The space went deeper though. Travis was taller and he was peering in like he'd spotted something. "What do you see?"

"Not sure. There's something in there, but it's too dark to make out." He reached in and felt around. "Some kind of box."

"Get it."

He pulled it out, staring at the dark green box just as hard as she was. It was about the size of a small tacklebox. Or an old-fashioned money box. He glanced up at her. "Breakfast room?"

She nodded, barely able to breathe with the weighty anticipation of knowing what was in there.

Gulf Coast Secrets

He carried the box down the hall and into the airy breakfast room where he set it on the table. "You open it. This is your aunt's stuff."

"Okay." She flipped the little clasp and lifted the lid.

The inside had a large main area but also a smaller divided shelf at the top that moved with the lid. It was about a third of the width of the box and would have held change. Those smaller compartments now held a few gold coins, a man's gold wedding band, a scarab beetle carved out of some kind of stone, and a silver cross on a chain.

Inside the main section was a stack of letters still in their envelopes and tied with a piece of white ribbon, some folded legal-looking paperwork, a bunch of old photographs in both black and white and color, and some other bits and bobs.

She stared into the box. "None of that really looks like anything we could use."

"I'm not so sure. We need to look at them closer." He picked up the stack of letters and riffled through the corner of them like a deck of playing cards. "I think these are all from Cecil. So probably nothing there."

She picked up the legal paperwork. "And these look like her divorce decrees." She moved on to the photographs. She shook her head as she went through them. "I don't even recognize most of these people. Or any of them really."

She was halfway through the pictures when she stopped and focused on the one in front of her. "This is odd. Did Norma have a facelift?"

"Not that I know of."

"Never mind, this isn't Norma in these pictures. But I don't know who this woman is. Or why my aunt would have pictures of her. Hard to say who she might be with that hat and big sunglasses. Is she a celebrity?"

He held his hand out. "May I?"

"Sure." She gave him the pictures.

He stared at the top photograph for a moment, then started shaking his head. "That's a celebrity all right."

"It is?" Georgia looked closer. "Which one?"

"The one who lives right here in Blackbird Beach. Lavinia Major."

"What? Are you serious? Lavinia had a facelift and Norma got pictures of the proof? That's some old school grudge holding right there."

"You're right, it is. I don't know how Norma got these. Or when Lavinia would have done this. If she'd been seen around town looking like this, it would have spread like wildfire. And I could be wrong, but I swear I remember there being a rumor she'd had work done but she made a public statement denying it and saying she'd sue anyone who perpetuated the lie."

Georgia's brows lifted. "If this really is Lavinia then my aunt sure knew what would push her buttons. Hard to sue anyone when there's irrefutable proof."

Travis tapped the photos against his hand. "I bet Lavinia would go to great lengths not to let these pictures get out."

"But there's no leverage unless we know this is really her. There had to be a time when she was away to have this done. A time we can prove. Unless there's a plastic surgeon in town?"

"In Blackbird Beach? We're lucky to have a dentist."

Gulf Coast Secrets

"So she would have had to travel. And then hide herself away for the recovery, which would have been a pretty reasonable amount of time. You don't recover from a facelift overnight."

"How long does it take?"

"I'm not even remotely an expert. I have no idea. All I know is it's major surgery. Look at the way she's bandaged up. And you can see the bruises peeking out. Let's see what Google says." Georgia took out her phone and called up the internet. A little typing and she had an answer. She read off the screen. "Seems like a minimum of four weeks before a person would look normal enough not to be noticeable."

She looked at Travis. "Four weeks is a long time to hide away without anyone remembering it. Maybe she made up an excuse. Like a long cruise. Or going away to visit a relative. Oh! Maybe she went to Alabama and had it done there. She could have stayed with Jillian?"

"Beats me. But then I don't exactly keep track of her social calendar. In fact, I see Lavinia as little as possible and have tried to keep it that way for a long time."

"I don't blame you." Georgia started thinking as a smile curved her mouth. "I bet there's a group of women who would know, however."

"Mia and the bridge club." He nodded. "I'll drive."

Georgia stuck the photos in her purse, and they were out the door. As soon as Georgia had her seatbelt on, she called Mia.

She answered right away. "Hey, Mom. Find anything yet?"

"I did but I need to talk to Agatha and her crew about it. Are you still with them? And where are you?"

Maggie Miller

"I am and we're at the thrift shop, in the storeroom. It's bigger than it sounds. I'll tell them you're on the way. They're excited to meet you."

Georgia smiled. "I'm excited to meet them too. Travis is with me. We'll see you in about ten minutes." She looked at Travis. He nodded. "Yep, ten minutes."

When they got to the shop, Travis had to park a block away because of the cars already at the curb. She recognized Griffin's car as one of them, but then he was in the Gazette doing his own research with Kelly. At least that's what Georgia hoped. Help from the newspaper's editor might be crucial.

They got out, Travis locked the truck, and they walked to the shop.

As they went inside, a little bell jangled over the door. Georgia looked around. "Mia? We're here, honey."

Mia came out from a door in the back wall. "Hey Mom, hey Travis. Back here."

Georgia and Travis walked to where she was. Mia held open the door marked employees only. "Come on in."

They walked through and found a large, mostly empty space with racks of clothes and shelves of donated merchandise. In the open space closest to them was one woman standing and three more sitting in folding chairs in a little circle. Nearby was a long table that held a coffee machine and all the fixings for that coffee, along with a mini fridge. There was also an open box of doughnuts from Ludlow's bakery that had about six left of the dozen it had once held.

Georgia raised her hand in greeting. "Hello, ladies."

They all smiled and greeted her in return.

Gulf Coast Secrets

Mia held her hand toward the older woman who was standing. "Mom, Travis, this is Agatha Goodwin. She runs the shop."

"And sings in the choir at church, which is where we know each other from," Travis said. He smiled. "Hi, Ms. Goodwin."

"Hello, Travis." Then she held her hand out to Georgia. "It's such a pleasure to meet you. Georgia, right?"

"Right." As soon as Georgia took Agatha's hand, the older woman clasped it between both of hers. "It's a pleasure to meet you, too."

Agatha held onto her. "Your great aunt was a dear friend to us. We are happy to help in whatever way we can."

Then, still holding onto Georgia with one hand, she turned. "This is Mary Lou Lebinski, Hilda Brant, and Ellen Chang. Ellen was our alternate until your aunt passed and then she took Norma's spot. Pearline over at City Hall is our alternate now."

Mary Lou had spiky silver-white hair and bright red lipstick that clashed wonderfully with her purple caftan and sparkly purple orthopedic shoes.

Hilda was dressed more conservatively in a sundress and cardigan, but a tattooed rose peeked a few petals out over the righthand neckline of the dress. Her steely gray hair was pulled back in a loose braid, allowing a few wisps to escape.

And Ellen, who seemed to be the youngest of the four, had a pristine brunette bob and perfect make up with clothes to match. It was the kind of polish that made Georgia wonder if she'd been a pageant girl. Only the faintest streaks of gray showed in her hair.

Maggie Miller

Georgia liked all of them immediately. "Nice to meet you all."

Agatha finally let go of Georgia's hand to do introductions. "Mary Lou owns the shell and crystal shop on Dolphin Drive."

Mary Lou nodded. "I always used to do a nice business with guests from the inn. Norma gave them a ten percent off coupon from me."

"I'd be happy to do that again," Georgia said, earning a bigger smile and a nod from Mary Lou.

Agatha went on. "Hilda's late husband was one of Blackbird Beach's mayors. She's the current president of the garden club."

"I'd love to talk to you about the window boxes at the inn," Georgia said. "Any advice you can give me on what to plant in them would be greatly appreciated."

"Of course," Hilda said. "Happy to do it."

Lastly, Agatha gestured to Ellen. "If Ellen looks familiar it's because she hosts *Wake Up, Blackbirds,* the town's morning show on local access channel thirteen. Before she moved here from New York, she was an anchorwoman."

That explained her look, Georgia thought. She had television polish.

Ellen shook her head. "They canned me because they said they were going in a different direction. That direction was younger." She rolled her eyes. "Not that I'm bitter." Then she laughed. "Losers."

Georgia snorted. She couldn't imagine a better group to help her with the task at hand. But she knew she'd have to repay them. She just didn't know how. Letting them use the space at the inn to play bridge didn't seem like enough, but at least it was something.

"Where do you play bridge now?" Georgia asked Agatha.

"We use the church rec hall sometimes," Agatha said. "But we just don't play as much as we used to. We tried playing here but it's not a comfortable spot."

Georgia gave them all her most hopeful smile. "I'd be happy to welcome you back to the inn very soon. But that all depends on what happens at the council meeting tomorrow. And much of that depends on how you can help me right now."

Maggie Miller

Chapter Twenty-one

Hilda nodded. "Whatever you need. I'm all for bringing Lavinia down. Hard."

Mary Lou shot her a look. "Hilda."

"What? I am." Hilda crossed her arms. "Maybe it's not very Christian, but you know how I feel about her." She looked at Georgia. "When my Archie passed, someone raised the idea of putting a plaque on one of the park benches in his honor. He was the mayor for twelve years, after all."

"And a good one," Ellen said.

Hilda smiled at her for a moment before continuing. "Thank you, Ellen. Lavinia shot it down because she said we'd have to make one up for every past mayor and it wasn't in the budget."

Travis snorted. "If the suggestion had been a plaque in her name, it would have been approved immediately and gold plated."

Agatha nodded. "Absolutely true."

Maggie Miller

"So," Mary Lou said as she gazed up at Georgia. "How can we help? Do you have a plan?"

"The beginnings of one," Georgia said. "But I need to flesh it out. Do any of you remember a time that Lavinia might have been away for about a month? Or if not away, then just out of sight?"

They all stared at her with their thinking faces on.

Travis stuck his hands in his pockets and rocked back on his heels. "Probably about ten years ago. Give or take."

Georgia let another few moments of silence go by, then tossed another clue into the mix. "She would have been in hiding to heal from a facelift."

All four women gasped, but Ellen spoke first. "I knew it. No one looks like that at her age without some help."

"I don't know." Mary Lou shook her head. "That's supposed to be just a rumor and we're not allowed to speak of it or she-who-shall-not-be-named will get sue happy."

"Lavoldermort can suck it," Hilda said.

Mia snickered. "Ten points to Gryffindor."

Looking pleased that her Harry Potter reference had been understood, Hilda glanced at Georgia. "Sadly, Mary Lou's right. The facelift is just a rumor."

"No, it's not." Georgia reached into her purse. "And I have proof."

She pulled the photos out and held them up.

Four new gasps greeted the pictures, along with open mouths and wide eyes.

Mia whistled. "Where did you get those, Mom?"

"Yes," Agatha said. "Where did you get them?"

Gulf Coast Secrets

"Norma had them stashed away. I suppose for a rainy day. And we're in the middle of a storm." She handed the pictures over to Agatha for closer inspection. "I have no idea how Norma got them or how she knew what Lavinia was up to but take a look for yourself and see if that's not Lavinia."

Agatha held on to one of the pictures but passed the rest to the other women. "That's her all right. But if you have these, why do you need us?"

"Because this isn't enough. I want to have the complete story. I need dates for when she would have done this. I'd love to know who her doctor was, too, but that's probably asking too much. The point is, telling her I have photos won't make as much impact as if I tell her I also know when it all happened and what the details were. Or at least as many details as I can come up with."

"Hang on, Mom," Mia said. "I don't think you should be the one to have that conversation with her."

"Why not?"

"For one thing, it feels kind of like blackmail and that's not something you want to get attached to."

"She's got a point," Travis said. "But I also know this could be what determines your future with the inn. If you think Lavinia will suddenly change her mind and grant you a new allowance out of the goodness of her heart, you don't know Lavinia."

The women all nodded. Agatha tugged at the hem of her sweater. "Lavinia will shut you down just as fast as she can, and she'll enjoy every moment of it. She won't have a hint of remorse."

Maggie Miller

"Well then..." Mia continued. "You at least need some distance from this. You can't be the one to bring the existence of this information to her."

Georgia thought about that. None of the women in front of her looked like they were about to volunteer, but she didn't expect them to. This wasn't really their fight and it wouldn't be fair of her to ask them to stick their necks out.

She looked at her daughter. "Then how do we do it?"

Mia didn't answer right away.

Travis, however, did. "I have an idea."

"I'm all ears."

"What if Norma had left those photos to a reliable source?"

"Such as?" Georgia asked.

"The one we're right next to." He stuck his hands in his pockets. "The Blackbird Gazette."

A slow smile spread across her face. "You're a smart man, Travis Taylor. A very smart man."

He grinned. "Thanks. Why don't you text Griffin, ask him how things are going and gauge the waters? I'd assume since he's still over there that Kelly was receptive to helping him, but it can't hurt to ask."

"Good thinking." She got her phone out. *How's it going?*

Griffin answered a moment later. *All right. Not finding anything yet.*

So Kelly's helping you?

Absolutely. No love for Lavinia.

Georgia looked up at Travis and nodded. "I'm going over." She looked at the group of women before her. "Ladies, it's been my pleasure to meet you and make your

Gulf Coast Secrets

acquaintance. I can't tell you how grateful I am for any help you can give us. Norma wouldn't back down from this fight and I'm not either. I understand, however, if you don't want to get involved further than this."

Mary Lou got to her feet. "I'm not going anywhere. Lavinia was a constant thorn in Norma's side. And Norma was a dear friend. Whatever you need me to do, just say it."

"Same here," Hilda said as she stood.

"Count me in as well." Ellen rose, smoothing her trousers. "In fact, I'm happy to cover the council meeting on my morning show. I don't have the broadest viewership, but anything I can do to spread the word about your victory, the better."

Georgia smiled. "You're assuming I'm going to win this thing. And I love that attitude, but I don't just need Lavinia to rescind that injunction, I need the council to grant me a new allowance. One in perpetuity that will keep the inn safe for as long as it exists. That feels like a lot to ask for in exchange for not sharing some information about a little plastic surgery."

Ellen shook her head, arms crossed. "You're underestimating the power of this town's distaste for that woman. Not to mention, I'm currently dating Jack Hannigan, who's also a councilman. One of my roast chicken dinners and he'll be amenable to voting for whatever I ask him to vote for."

Agatha snickered. "Ellen, that's awfully sly."

She shrugged. "We should have done something about Lavinia a long time ago."

Maggie Miller

"Very true," Hilda said. "The fact that she's giving you all this grief is at least partially on us."

"No," Georgia said. "I don't believe that for one bit."

Mary Lou sighed. "Hilda's right. We got complacent. Norma must be shaking her head at us. You go talk to that newspaper editor, see if she'll help you. But if she won't, you don't worry about it. We'll come up with something."

They passed the pictures back to Agatha.

"Thank you." Georgia smiled at all of them. "I'll be right back. In the meantime if you can think about what those dates might be?"

"We'll do our best," Agatha said. She handed the photographs back to Georgia.

"That's all I can ask." Georgia tucked the photos into her purse, then gave them a little wave and walked next door to the paper. Through the windows, she could see Griffin with Chloe on his shoulder. He was sitting next to Kelly at her desk, both of them peering intently at the computer screen.

For a moment, she had the strangest thought about how much they looked like a happy little family. She shook that off. Despite what she thought, she wasn't about to mention such a thing to her son. It was silly and a complication Griffin didn't need.

Even so, she hated to interrupt the moment. But she had no choice. The clock was ticking. Hoping she was making the right move, she went through the door.

Gulf Coast Secrets

Chapter Twenty-two

Griffin looked up. "Hey, Mom."

"Hi, honey. And hi again, Kelly."

Kelly pushed her glasses to the top of her head. "Hello, Mrs. Carpenter."

"I understand Griffin has told you what's going on."

She frowned. "He has. I'm so sorry."

"Thanks. Me, too." Georgia stood in front of the desk. "I have something pertaining to that matter that I'd like to talk to you about."

"Sure," Kelly stood and brought another chair over. "Please, have a seat."

Georgia sat, suddenly more nervous than she realized. "I understand you aren't exactly a Lavinia fan either."

"She's not my favorite person in town, no." Kelly sighed. "I probably shouldn't say that seeing as how I'm supposed to be an unbiased journalist, but I'm also a person who's had to deal with her…expectations. Anyway, what would you like to talk about?"

Maggie Miller

Georgia took a breath, a little tongue-tied. "I found something that might influence Lavinia's thinking about the injunction. And the new allowance we need to keep the third floor of the inn. But it's been suggested that I shouldn't be the one to share with her what I've found. That a more impartial third-party might be the way to go."

One side of Kelly's mouth ticked up a half-grin. "Such as myself?"

"Your name came up."

Kelly looked almost gleeful as she asked her next question. "What's this information? Off the record, of course."

"I have photographic evidence of something Lavinia has denied. Something she's apparently threatened to sue anyone for talking about, which as I understand it, has successfully killed the topic."

"Holy cow, Mom," Griffin said. "What did you find?"

Kelly nodded. "Yeah, I'm dying to know too."

Georgia reached into her purse, her fingers finding the photographs instantly. "The woman in these photos has been verified as Lavinia by a family member of hers. Former family member, I suppose I should say." Especially since Travis and Jillian were divorced.

Georgia took the pictures out and spread them across Kelly's desk.

She put her glasses on and stared at them. "That's a facelift if I ever saw one." She looked up at Georgia. "And I've seen one. My auntie, Prisha, had one. Same kind of bandages, same kind of bruises."

Gulf Coast Secrets

Then she shook her head. "I've never heard about this, though. I mean that Lavinia had had one but wouldn't own up to it."

"Well," Griffin said. "Clearly people believe her threat that she'll sue. And with her reputation, who would want to test that?"

Georgia nodded. "That's what I think too."

"What else were you thinking?" Kelly asked. "As far as how you want this handled?"

"Something along the lines of this: say Norma had actually left these photos to the paper along with money to publish them. Like an ad. What would you do in that case?"

Kelly thought about that. "I suppose I'd publish them, because if that's how this had really gone down I wouldn't have known that these photos were of Lavinia. Once you said it, however, I could absolutely identify her."

She picked up a pen and tapped it on the desk. "But that's not what happened. Norma didn't leave them to me. So I'd be more comfortable saying they came from an anonymous source."

That would point the finger a little more directly at Georgia, but she was okay with that. There wouldn't be any concrete proof. Just Lavinia's guess.

"All right. And just to make it really straight up, how much would it cost if I was going to publish them? Say a full page?"

Kelly took a sheet of paper from a little bin on the corner of her desk and set it in front of Georgia. "Here's our rate sheet. Black and white or color?"

"The photos are in color so..." Georgia drew her fingernail down the column to find the cost. "Okay. I'll write you a check for that much. Then you can honestly say you've been paid to publish the photos."

"Unless?"

"Unless she agrees to stop harassing Norma Merriweather's family and to grant the inn a lifetime allowance for the third floor."

Kelly nodded. "You think she'll go for it?"

"I have no idea. What do you think?"

Kelly moved the rate sheet to look at the photos once again. "I think Lavinia Major is a woman who cares more about what people think of her than anyone realizes. I also think she'd do just about anything to keep one of her lies from being exposed."

Georgia exhaled the breath she'd been holding. "If I can come up with any more details such as when this surgery took place, I'll let you know." She smiled and reached into her purse for her checkbook. "Do I make this out to the Gazette?"

"Mom, are you really going to do it if Lavinia doesn't back down?"

Georgia thought about that. Then thought about what Norma would do. "I don't know yet. But I have also yet to hear one decent thing the woman has done. If she destroys my best chance for a new beginning…I just might."

Griffin's brows shot up. "If that's what you decide, I stand behind you."

"Thanks, honey. I just can't let her steal this dream away from all of us without some kind of consequence. Maybe that's petty, but it's how I feel."

Gulf Coast Secrets

"There are a lot of people in this town who would think you were a hero," Kelly said.

"Well, that might be true, but I don't even want my name attached to this. Better she wonder who did it than know for sure."

"Agreed," Kelly said. "I'll have to do this right away seeing as how the meeting is tomorrow."

"Yes." Georgia leaned in a little. "Can I ask what you're going to do?"

"Sure. Simple. I'm going to call her in and tell her what's been given to me. Then I'm going to ask her if she'd like to confirm that's her in the photos. And let the conversation go from there."

Griffin rubbed Chloe's back. "Any chance I can be here while that happens? Lavinia doesn't know who I am."

"Yet," Kelly said. But then she nodded. "Actually, I think I'd prefer it. Just for security purposes. You can sit at one of those other desks and look busy. Maybe even with headphones on so she doesn't know you're listening in."

Georgia frowned. "Security purposes? You think Lavinia would try to hurt you?"

"No!" Kelly laughed. "But I wouldn't put it past her to grab the photos and try to tear them up."

"Oh. Good point. I should probably make copies of those."

"I'll do that right now for you." She took the photos over to the copier, arranged them on the glass plate, then closed the cover and tapped a few buttons on the side. "I'll make two, one for each of us. You can take a copy and the photos, and I'll keep a copy to show her."

Maggie Miller

"I appreciate that. Thank you," Georgia said.

Kelly came back and handed her the copy.

Georgia took it, then gathered up the photos as well.

"Mom," Griffin said. "You should probably take Chloe home with you."

"All right, I will. Let me just go check in with the girls and see if they've come up with a date for when this facelift might have happened, and I'll be back."

"Okay. Thanks." He kissed Chloe's downy little head, but she was fast asleep. "Oh, one more thing. Tell Travis I need to talk to him later."

"Will do." Georgia wondered if that was about Griff moving into Travis's cottage or something else, but she had too much on her mind already to give it a lot of thought. She put everything in her purse and went back to the thrift shop.

Travis and Mia had joined the circle of women and were both in the final stages of finishing a doughnut. Everyone looked at Georgia as she came in.

"How did it go?" Mia asked.

"Good. We have a plan." No clue if it would work, but it was worth a shot. "Did anyone figure out a date yet?"

"We did," Agatha said. "January, eight or nine years ago. We're still working out that detail."

Hilda nodded. "The more we talked about it, the more we started to remember. Lavinia made a big deal about going out west to see the Grand Canyon, but that was only about a ten-day trip."

"Then," Elle said. "I called Jack up and asked him if he could ever remember a time that she'd missed a council meeting. He said yes, once. Right after her trip out west."

Gulf Coast Secrets

Mary Lou's eyes narrowed. "She claimed to have come down with a terrible cold, caught on the airplane."

Agatha shook her head. "Which reminded me of a thing that happened to Eloise, one of the ladies from church. She made soup for Lavinia. But when she took it to her house, Lavinia wouldn't let her in. Wouldn't do much more than shout through the door at her. Eloise never even saw her."

Mia's brows lifted with obvious excitement. "We just can't figure out if that was eight years ago or nine. But pretty good right?"

"Very good." Georgia looked at Travis. "You don't remember her going on that trip?"

He shook his head with seeming disappointment. "No, but if it happened around when Jillian left or around when all of the divorce stuff was going on I wouldn't have realized it. I was pretty actively avoiding Lavinia during that time. She could have painted herself blue and I wouldn't have noticed."

"Wait." An inkling of an idea popped into her head. "I think I know how to figure this out."

Georgia whipped out her phone and dialed Griffin.

He answered on the third ring. "Did you figure out a date?"

"Maybe. Does Kelly have a way to search subscribers' accounts to see when they might have put their delivery on hold?"

"Hang on, I'll ask her."

She could hear him doing just that but couldn't quite make out Kelly's answer.

"Yes," he said. "How far back?"

"Eight or nine years?"

He relayed that information, then spoke to his mother again. "She can only go back about five years. That's when she took over and the new system was installed."

Georgia sighed. "Hmm, all right. Never mind. The girls think the date of the facelift is about eight or nine years ago in January. They just can't remember which."

"Oh. Well, I'll tell her anyway. Hey, it's still good information. You have a month."

"True. I'll be over in a few to pick up Chloe."

"See you then."

She hung up and shook her head. "The Gazette's records don't go back that far." She shrugged as she smiled. "Thank you again for all your help and your support. It was so nice to meet you all and know that you were such good friends of my aunt's. And now, I hope, good friends of mine as well."

"You betcha." Agatha nodded. "We'll see you tomorrow night at the council meeting. If anything happens before then…"

Mia gave her a thumbs up. "I'll call you, don't you worry." She waved. "Bye, ladies."

They all waved back. "Bye."

Travis held the door for Georgia and Mia, and they walked out together.

On the sidewalk, Mia squinted into the sun. "See you back at the house?"

"Yes. I told Griffin that I'd take Chloe home for him. He's going to stay and be a fly on the wall while Kelly talks to Lavinia.

"Ooo," Mia said. "So jealous. But you're in Travis's truck, right?"

Gulf Coast Secrets

Travis nodded. "We are. Why?"

"Because it would be easier for me to just swap cars with Griff. Because of the car seat."

"I totally forgot about that," Georgia said. "Some Mimi I am."

Travis laughed. "You'll get there. Thanks, Mia."

"Sure."

"Wait," Georgia said. "Travis, Griffin also wanted to talk to you about something. Although he didn't say when."

Travis shrugged. "Why not now? With that injunction in place, it's not like I can go back and work on the inn."

Maggie Miller

Gulf Coast Secrets

Chapter Twenty-three

Travis held the door again for Georgia and Mia as they all went into the Gazette.

Griffin was at one of the smaller desks, working on the computer. Chloe was asleep in her carrier on the desk that was next to his.

Kelly was sitting at the microfiche machine. Travis was impressed that the paper had one, but even more impressed that Kelly knew how to use it. Then again, he supposed her father wouldn't have made such an investment in her if she hadn't been intelligent enough to do the job of editor.

Kelly turned to look up at them over the rim of her glasses and smiled. "Eight years. It was eight years ago. In January."

"How did you figure it out?" Georgia asked.

"On a hunch I decided to look at old issues of the Gazette. I might not have all of the past records on the computer, but I have all the past issues on microfiche. So I started looking through them to see what I could find. And it paid off." She turned back to the machine, pushing her glasses into place.

Maggie Miller

She pointed to the screen. "In the About Town section. *Lavinia Major leaves today on an extensive tour of the great American West. She hopes to see the Grand Canyon as well as Hoover Dam. We wish her a safe trip and a speedy return.*"

"Well done," Georgia said.

"Thanks," Kelly said. "I wouldn't be much of a journalist if I couldn't do a little investigative work now and then."

"Have you reached out to Lavinia yet?" Georgia asked.

Kelly shook her head. "No, but I'm about to call her."

Travis stuck his hands in his pockets. "We'll be out of your hair soon." He looked at Griffin. "You wanted to see me?"

Griffin glanced at Kelly, then back at Travis. "I did. But we could talk later."

Travis shrugged. "I don't have much else to do with that injunction hanging over us, so unless you're busy, I don't mind talking now."

"Okay." Griffin seemed reluctant, but Travis didn't understand why. It was his idea to talk.

Mia held her hand out with her car keys in it. "First, give me your keys and my adorable niece. I'll take her home in your car since you already have the car seat in there. You can drive my car when you're ready to leave."

"Good thinking." Griffin fished his keys out of his pocket, then carefully picked up the carrier and brought it to Mia. "You know how to connect this to the car seat?"

"Yep. I used to babysit, remember?" She took his keys as he took hers.

"Yeah, but it's not like you were driving the kids around."

"Whatever. I can do it."

Gulf Coast Secrets

He made a face. "I'll help you." He looked at Travis. "We can talk outside, if that's okay."

"Sure. I'll be out when your mom is ready to go."

"Okay." Griffin and Mia went outside.

"I'm ready," Georgia said. "Unless you need me for anything else, Kelly?"

Kelly shook her head. "I've got everything I need now."

Georgia smiled. "Thanks again."

"Thank *you*. Consider this a public service. Taking Lavinia down a notch will be good for everyone."

With a laugh, Georgia walked out with Travis.

Griffin was finishing up with the car seat. He kissed Chloe goodbye, then carefully shut the car door and gave his sister a look. "Drive safely. That's precious cargo in there."

"I know. And I'm a very safe driver, so calm down." Mia got behind the wheel, waved at them, then pulled away from the curb.

Griffin came to stand by Travis and Georgia on the sidewalk.

Travis could tell by the look in Griffin's eyes and his body language that he was reluctant to talk, even though he was the one who'd wanted the conversation. "What's on your mind, son?"

Griffin exhaled and ran his hand through his hair. "I sort of told Kelly that if she'd help us with this Lavinia thing, I'd find someone to run against her in the next council election. Which is next month. She's running unopposed."

"She always does," Travis added. "I don't think anyone's willing to test those waters. The backlash could be pretty strong."

"Well, Kelly said the paper would endorse whoever ran. And that would help, right?"

"It would," Travis said. "I think it might help a lot."

"And if Kelly can make Lavinia realize she's not untouchable...that might make a difference, too."

"It would probably shake her pretty good," Travis agreed.

Griffin swallowed. "So what do you think?"

"Oh." Travis wracked his brain as he realized Griffin wanted suggestions. "Um, how about Andy Crenshaw who owns the hardware store? He might run against her. Or Lester Venable. Or even his wife, Susan. Although they're pretty busy with the dry cleaners—"

"No," Griffin said. "I meant you. I told Kelly I'd ask you."

Travis stared at him. "Me?"

"That's a great idea," Georgia said.

Travis raised his hands. "Hold on, now."

"Why?" Georgia looked far too happy about this new idea. "You'd be perfect. You're local and well-liked, and you'd have all kinds of support. We could help you campaign and host a party at the inn—"

"Just a second," Travis said. "You're putting the cart before the horse. For one thing, the election is next month. You don't even know if you'll have an inn by then."

"Faith, Travis. And there are other places to hold campaign parties." She looked at her son. "I love the idea."

Griffin sighed. "Thanks, but the potential candidate has yet to agree."

"Can I think about it? It's a big ask." But Travis already was thinking about it. Running against Lavinia was a fool's errand, but if he could actually win…that would be something for the record books.

Just to see the look on Lavinia's face would be worth the aggravation.

"Sure," Griffin said. "Think all you want. I really don't mean to push you into anything. You just seemed like such a great choice."

"You think so?"

Griffin nodded. "I haven't known you long, but I already know you're a stand-up guy. My aunt certainly thought highly of you. You're exactly the sort of guy that should be looking after this town and its citizens."

"That's kind of you." Travis smiled a little. "I promise to give it real thought. But maybe we should see how the council meeting comes out first."

Griffin looked a little downcast, but Travis wasn't about to commit to something on the spot that was such a big deal. Griffin nodded. "Okay. I'll see you at the house later. Hopefully with a good report on Lavinia's visit."

Georgia patted his arm. "See you later, honey."

Travis walked her to the truck, opened her door, then went around to the drivers' side. He got in and got them on the road. His mind was going a hundred miles an hour, but he kept the truck to the speed limit.

"He's right, you know."

He glanced over at her, having only half-heard her comment. "What's that?"

"Griffin. He's right. You'd be a great councilman."

He shook his head. "I don't know. Those people are all…"

"All what?"

He frowned. "College educated, for one thing."

"That doesn't mean anything."

He cut his eyes at her. "Yes, it does."

"Nope. It does not. And you're not going to convince me otherwise."

He almost laughed. "You're very cute when you're stubborn."

"I'm not being cute. I'm being serious. Stop trying to change the subject."

"You're still cute."

She gave him a stern look.

"I bet you used to look at your kids like that."

Her lower lip quivered, then she laughed out loud. "You make it very hard to have a serious conversation."

"Sorry."

"You're still smirking."

"Am I?" He laughed. "I really will think about it."

"What worries you about the idea?"

He paused to dig into that question. But the answer came to him pretty quickly. "That she'll bring up my past. Say I was an unfit father."

"But that's not true. Don't people around here know what really happened?"

"Some do. Some don't. Most won't care. They'll just see the picture of me that Lavinia paints and think it's the truth."

Georgia sighed. "We'll have to prove them wrong."

"How?"

"Better campaigning."

"I don't want to play dirty."

Gulf Coast Secrets

"I don't think there's any need to. Although Lavinia probably will."

"Then let her. I don't want to go down that road."

She grinned. "So you'll run a nice, honorable campaign."

"Exactly."

She was still grinning.

"What?"

"I'm just happy."

"About?"

She laughed softly. "You deciding to run."

Maggie Miller

Gulf Coast Secrets

Chapter Twenty-four

Griffin knew the plan. Sit at the desk in the corner with headphones on and act like he was working. He would be, too. Sort of.

He was working on setting up a seller's account for himself on one of the many stock photo sites. Might not bring in much money, but there was no end to the beautiful beach shots available and someone might want to buy them. He planned on adding some of his other, older photos too, but he had a feeling the beach pictures would do the best.

None of that was super important immediately, however because setting up the account was mostly just busy work that would allow him to look active while he was really listening in on Kelly and Lavinia's conversation.

Based on Kelly's phone call with Lavinia, her arrival was imminent.

"Are you nervous?" Griffin asked his boss.

"A little," Kelly answered. "But energized too. I feel like this is something that needs to be done. Lavinia has been the town bully too long. I just don't know if she's going to react the way I hope she does."

"Which is to back down?"

Kelly nodded. "I don't know if she has that in her."

"Will you really publish the photos?"

"I will. I won't put a name on them, which will prevent her from claiming defamation or libel, but her name won't be necessary anyway. Lavinia's lived in Blackbird Beach long enough to be recognizable."

"What if she sues?"

"She'll have no legal footing. But hey, if she wants to waste her money, she can." Kelly's gaze shifted from him to something outside the windows. "She's here."

He looked and saw a black Mercedes sedan pull up to the curb. He put his headphones on and faced the screen. He moved his head slightly, like he was caught up in the beat of his music. He figured if he was going to act, might as well make it Oscar-worthy.

Lavinia charged through the front door. "All right, Kelly. I'm here. What's so important you needed to see me immediately?"

"Good afternoon to you, too, Lavinia."

Griffin was faced away from the two women, but he could easily see them in the reflection on his screen.

Lavinia almost rolled her eyes. "Good afternoon, Kelly. What did you want to see me about? I'm a busy woman, you know."

"Aren't we all?" Kelly was playing it cool and calm. Which only seemed to irritate Lavinia more.

Griffin had to work at not laughing.

Gulf Coast Secrets

Kelly reached for the file she'd left on her desk. The one with the photos in it. She opened it just enough to grab one of the pictures, took one out and held it up. "Can you confirm that this is a photograph of you?"

"What?" Lavinia dug into her purse for her reading glasses, promptly shoving them onto her face. She reached out to take the photo, but Kelly pulled it just out of her grasp.

"This is a look only situation," Kelly said. "So. Is this you?" She asked again. "I have others if you'd like to see a different angle."

Lavinia squinted at the picture. Then her jaw went slack, and her eyes widened. "Where did you get that?"

"Then it is you?"

"I didn't say that. Where did you get that?" Lavinia's tone had taken on a hint of threat, but there was panic in it too.

He stared harder at his screen, doing his best to disappear.

"If it's not you, why does it matter where it came from?"

"Where?" Lavinia repeated. "Tell me."

Kelly slipped the photo back into the folder. "Photos were provided to the paper with the instructions that they were to be published with your name and the date of January. Eight years ago to be exact. When you were supposedly visiting the Grand Canyon. Remember that? Pretty easy to verify. It was in the About Town section of the Gazette. I can print you a copy if you'd like."

Lavinia looked apoplectic. There was a vein in her forehead that was clearly visible, making Griffin wonder if she was about to ruin that long-ago facelift with new wrinkles. "I was…out west then."

"Were you? Because I'm pretty sure one of the photos has a palm tree in it. Looks a lot like Florida if you ask me."

"Who gave you those photos?"

"I'm not at liberty to say. But…" Kelly pressed her index finger against the folder and stared at it meaningfully before responding to Lavinia. "It's possible something you did triggered their arrival."

"What is that supposed to – *Norma*." Lavinia snarled his aunt's name like it was a curse word.

"I'm sorry?" Kelly asked, as if she didn't understand.

"Don't play dumb with me." Lavinia had apparently dropped all pretense of being nice. Not that she'd been doing such a great job of it to begin with.

Kelly crossed her arms. "In what way am I playing dumb? If you think Norma Merriweather is behind this, you must have good reason." Kelly leaned in. "You do know she's deceased, right?"

"Don't—" Lavinia grimaced. "It wouldn't be beyond her to have some kind of clause in her will to attack me if I took an action she didn't like."

Griffin pursed his lips to keep from smiling. This was going better than he'd expected.

"What action have you taken that Norma wouldn't like?" Kelly prodded.

"You know very well. The injunction. Against the inn."

"Hmm. You're right. I don't think Norma would like that, would she? You attacking her family that way, trying to ruin their chance at reopening the inn, and at making a life for themselves here…that's pretty awful. Even for you. And I didn't even mention how helpful reopening the inn would be

Gulf Coast Secrets

to the businesses in town that benefit from the tourist dollars."

Lavinia's eyes narrowed. "Are you in on this?"

"In on what? An attempt to make you behave with a little human decency?"

Griffin almost choked. Kelly wasn't holding back. And it was making him fall in love with her just a little bit.

Lavinia huffed. "I wouldn't put it past you. I know you don't like me."

Kelly laughed. "Why would I like you? You've extorted free ads from my business for years now, which has cost the paper a sizable income that I could have used to hire more employees. In essence, your behavior has caused fewer jobs in this town. That's not very likable behavior, is it?"

"I am *bringing* you *business*."

"You keep telling yourself that." Then Kelly stared at her for a long moment without saying a word. "The photos will be in the next edition. Have a good day."

Lavinia appeared to be trembling. He wanted to look at her, but he didn't dare move.

"You can't publish those," Lavinia said quietly.

Had Kelly broken her? Griffin doubted it. The woman didn't seem breakable.

"I absolutely can. The ad's already been paid for." Kelly let out a light laugh. "Hey, I guess you *did* bring me business."

"No, you can't do this."

"Why not?"

"I'll sue you."

"On what grounds?"

"Slander."

Kelly picked up the folder. "Slander refers to a spoken statement."

Lavinia rolled her eyes. "Libel then. Whatever, my attorney will know."

"Then he or she will probably also know libel refers to false written or published statements." Kelly tapped the folder in her arms. "But these are pictures of you and your name won't be on them, so what's false about them?"

Maybe it was a weird reflection on his screen, but Griff could swear there was steam coming out of Lavinia's ears.

Kelly tipped her head to one side like she was considering something. "I *suppose* I could be convinced not to publish these."

"How?" Lavinia asked the question almost before Kelly had finished speaking.

"You could drop the injunction. Grant the inn the necessary allowance to keep its third floor and be fully operational. You know, that sort of thing."

"That's...that's..."

"Extortion?" Kelly asked, with a sly, knowing look. "Tell you what. I'll come to the council meeting tomorrow night and see what kind of decisions get made. Then I'll make one of my own. How does that sound?"

If Lavinia glared any harder, she'd probably pop an eyeball out of its socket. "This isn't over."

"Correct," Kelly said. "That's what I was just explaining. You have until tomorrow night to do the right thing. Then I'll have to decide what's best for the town."

Lavinia just stomped toward the door.

"Oh," Kelly called out. "One more thing."

"What?" Lavinia snapped.
"Your free ads are over."

Maggie Miller

Gulf Coast Secrets

Chapter Twenty-five

Georgia was a mess. A nervous wreck of worry with occasional bouts of frustration, righteous indignation, and revenge fantasies.

"Mom," Mia said. "Have a glass of wine and come sit on the back porch. You're wearing a path in the flooring."

"She's right," Travis said. "There isn't anything you can do. Twisting yourself up over this is going to give you an ulcer."

She stopped pacing. "This is our life at stake."

He nodded. "I know. But don't ruin your health over it."

Mia went to the kitchen. "I'm getting the wine out and I'm pouring us both a glass. Travis, you want a beer?"

"Yes, thank you." He walked up to Georgia and took hold of her hands. "Whatever happens, you're going to be okay."

"Thanks. Why don't I feel that way? All of a sudden I can't shake the sense that something dark is creeping over me."

"It's just nerves."

"Mom, Griffin is pulling in."

Maggie Miller

Georgia took a breath and turned toward the door.

Mia came out from the kitchen and handed her a glass of wine. "Regardless of what he tells us, you're going to want this."

"Thanks." She wasn't wrong. Georgia took a sip. A big sip.

Then Mia handed Travis a beer, giving him a hopeful smile.

Griffin walked through the door, immediately looking around. "Where's Chloe?"

"Sleeping in the Pack-n-Play," Mia answered. "Come into the living room and tell us everything."

"Okay."

He looked happy. Well, at least pleased, Georgia thought. She went into the living room with all of them. They filled almost every seat.

He shook his head. "For one thing, Kelly Singh is amazing."

"What happened?" Mia asked. "Did Lavinia admit those photos were of her?"

"Not in so many words. But it was pretty clear she knew that they were. And she figured out they came from Norma."

"So?" Georgia asked breathlessly. "Is she going to rescind the injunction?"

Griffin made a face. "I don't know. She wouldn't say. But Kelly made it clear that if things don't get straightened out at the council meeting, the photos would be in the next edition of the paper."

Some of Georgia's anxiety lifted. "We'll still need the allowance, though."

Gulf Coast Secrets

He shook his head. "No, Kelly made that part of the deal. She's no dummy, that one."

"No, she isn't," Travis said.

Mia sat back. "You should have invited Kelly over for dinner."

"I did," Griffin said. "But she already had plans with her family. What are we having for dinner? I'm hungry."

Georgia shook her head. "I haven't even thought about it."

Travis looked at her. "Do you mind if I take over your kitchen?"

"And make dinner?"

He nodded. "I can cook, you know. How do you think I've kept myself alive all these years?"

She smiled. "Sure, do whatever you want in there. I don't have much of an appetite anyway."

"You want help?" Mia asked.

"I'd love some."

He and Mia went into the kitchen, leaving Georgia with her son.

"Do you think Lavinia's going to comply?"

Griffin nodded right away. "She seemed pretty adamant that those photos do not get published."

"I hope you're right."

"Mom, you can still appeal the injunction."

"But Roger said it was written into the contract in such a way that we'd have a hard time getting it overturned."

"Okay, but how about the fact that it's causing you personal harm? Loss of income? There has to be something."

He shook his head. "Doesn't matter, this is all going to be over tomorrow night, and we'll be back to work."

"And if that's not how things go…"

"It will."

She appreciated her son's enthusiasm, but life had taught her to be realistic and prepare for any eventuality. "If it's not. Then there is a good chunk of money left in the account Norma left me. That plus whatever I can get for selling the inn—"

"You'd sell the inn?" He looked stricken.

"Well, if I can't operate it what else can I do with it? I can't afford to keep it. And that property is very valuable."

"But that means someone would buy it to tear it down."

She nodded, unable to speak or do anything else but stare at her hands and think about Norma's inn. The one that was supposed to be her and Cecil's dream house. Losing that would be like losing Norma all over again.

"No," he said. "That can't happen."

She shook her head. "I don't want that either."

"Maybe…if things don't go our way, and Travis runs for her seat and wins, maybe then we could overturn it."

Georgia picked her head up. "I hadn't thought about that. But again, that's a lot of ifs and maybes."

"But it's still a chance." He smiled at her. "Don't lose hope, Mom. I really think we've got this."

"Good." Georgia made herself smile back although she didn't really feel it.

Griffin put his hands on the arms of the chair like he was about to get up. "I should feed Chloe. Are you going to be all right if I leave you alone?"

Gulf Coast Secrets

She was touched by his concern. Enough that her smile turned genuine. "I'm fine. Go take care of that sweet baby."

"Okay." He went into the bedroom.

She took another sip of her wine and stared out at the beach. That's what she needed. A walk to clear her head.

She carried her wine into the kitchen, where a flurry of activity was going on. Clyde was watching from the safe distance of a chair. "Do I have time for a walk on the beach?"

Travis turned. He'd tucked a kitchen towel into the waistband of his jeans like an apron. It was somehow endearing and sexy. "Absolutely. We're about twenty-five minutes out. Or do you want me to push it back further?"

"Nope, that's plenty. I'll be back by then." She finished her wine, set the glass by the sink, then tucked her phone into the back pocket of her jeans and slipped out the rear sliders. She stood on the deck for a moment, just breathing the salt air.

Already she felt better. Although some of that might have been the wine.

She toed off her flats and walked barefoot onto the sandy path. There was something about connecting herself to the earth like that that lifted her spirits. It was almost like being a child again when her cares had been few and far in between.

She walked straight down to the water. The waves rolled in, lapping the sand, the sound relaxing her. She stuck her hands in the pockets of her jeans and just stared out at the horizon. The sun was sinking, gilding the water with a golden glow.

A few of the clouds were tinted pink and here and there, streaks of peach colored the sky. She was once again reminded of how beautiful this place was. She didn't want to leave it. She couldn't leave it. Not without a fight.

But how much fight did she have in her?

One of the waves reached her toes. She glanced down at the foam left behind. The bubbles popped, disappearing quickly. She wasn't her aunt. She didn't have Norma's confidence or backbone, no matter how much she tried to be that kind of woman.

So again the question filled her head. How much fight did she have in her?

For herself, maybe not that much. But this wasn't just about her. This was about her children. And Travis, too. There was no way she could leave him out of this, not when he'd been such a big part of Norma's life.

She walked south for a little bit, keeping her pace slow and watching the sand to make sure she didn't step on anything she shouldn't. Once in a while, there were jelly fish. Or the sharp edges of broken shells.

Broken shells were everywhere, but so were whole ones. The beach was scattered with them, but there was no sea glass in sight this time.

She kept going, kept thinking. Whatever happened tomorrow night, she couldn't let that be the end of it. Not without exhausting every possibility. She lifted her head to watch a seagull fly by. She'd been through plenty of hard times before, what was one more?

If that meant sticking around and trying to help Travis win his campaign against Lavinia, then so be it. She stopped walking. What if Travis really could win? That would be

Gulf Coast Secrets

something, wouldn't it? She turned and headed back to the cottage, but this time she was smiling.

As she walked, she ran through all the scenarios of what might happen in her head. A few more steps and she stopped again, realizing she was directly in front of the inn. She gazed at it, imagining what it would look like bustling with guests and activity.

She wanted to see that for real. She *would* see it for real. If there had ever been a time to fight, this was it. She started walking toward the cottage again. Up ahead, a frosted piece of pale green sea glass caught her eye. She scooped it up.

Georgia had no choice but to fight. She had too much to lose.

Maggie Miller

Gulf Coast Secrets

Chapter Twenty-six

Mia looked up from setting the table to see her mom and brother walk in from the back deck. Griffin had gone out there to sit and relax after feeding Chloe and was still carrying her on his shoulder. "Hey, Mom. How was your walk?"

Georgia smiled. "It was great. I really needed that."

Mia had no doubts about that. Her mom had been looking pretty stressed. Now she seemed more like herself. "Well, you're just in time for dinner."

Georgia strolled into the kitchen with Griffin behind her. "I just want you all to know that whatever happens tomorrow night, I'm not giving up. I'm going to fight this until every option has been exhausted. I owe Norma that much."

Pride filled Mia. "I think that's great, Mom."

"Me, too," Griffin said. "I'm with you all the way."

"Same," Travis announced from his spot by the stove.

Georgia glanced at him. "It smells great in here, by the way. What are we having?"

Travis turned around, wiping his hands on a towel. "I don't know what to call it exactly. It's sort of like a mashup between fettuccine Alfredo and pasta Primavera with my own twist thrown in." He laughed. "It doesn't really have a name, but I promise it will taste fantastic."

Mia chuckled. "How about pasta ala Travis?"

"I'm good with that," he said.

Georgia shook her head. "Doesn't matter what it's called, I'll eat it. I'm starving."

Mia gave her mom a look. "Just a second ago you said you didn't have an appetite."

"I didn't. But that walk on the beach really fixed me up."

Not just her appetite, Mia thought. But her outlook too.

"Anything I can do to help?" Griffin asked.

Mia shook her head. "Nope. Well, you can get yourself a drink. Actually, you can get everybody drinks."

"Okay, let me put Chloe in her carrier."

"Water's fine for me," Georgia said.

"Same here," Travis said.

A few minutes later, they were all at the table with full plates before them.

"This looks great," Georgia said. "And not just because I didn't have to prepare it. But that definitely helped."

Mia laughed and agreed as she looked at her plate. Bow tie pasta in a creamy Alfredo sauce with peas, mushrooms, a little sundried tomato, and diced ham, which was actually Canadian bacon that had been on special at Ludlow's the day before. Travis had also sprinkled a little Cajun seasoning into the sauce. She added a shake of parmesan cheese, then passed the container to Griffin.

Gulf Coast Secrets

As they ate, they all seemed to make a conscious effort not to talk about Lavinia or the injunction or the town council meeting to come. It was as if they all knew they needed a break from those topics.

Instead, they talked about random things. Like Chloe needing a highchair. And how Ludlow's bakery was holding a contest to come up with a new cupcake flavor.

Then Griffin told them about the last job he'd been on. The one before the one he'd been fired from. He told them all about the beautiful location and the interesting clothes that he'd had to shoot for the fashion spread. He also told them about his decision to try to sell some of his photographs through a stock photo site.

Mia nodded. "I think that's a great idea. I mean, why not try to make a little extra money, right?"

Griffin picked up his glass of water and took a drink before answering. "That's what I was thinking."

"What are stock photos used for?" Travis asked.

"All kinds of things," Griffin said. "Advertisements, social media, blog posts, almost anywhere you see a picture. Some of those are from custom photo shoots, but a lot of them come from stock photo sites. And with the beach here being as beautiful as it is, I can't see why someone wouldn't want to use some of those pictures."

"I see," Travis said. "It is beautiful around here."

Mia glanced towards the back of the house. The bright golden glow of sunset streamed through the windows. "That reminds me, I should really get out there and see if I can get a sunset picture."

Georgia wiped her mouth and set her napkin on the table. "You absolutely should. How are the social media accounts going?"

"We get more followers every day," Mia answered. "Not tons, but they're trickling in. And I expect the Instagram account will blow up as soon as I get some shirtless Griffin paddle boarding pictures on there."

Griffin rolled his eyes. "Here we go with that again."

Travis laughed. "Sometimes you just have to do what you have to do. Take one for the team, as it were." He looked at Georgia and gave her a cute glance that made Mia wonder if something new was going on between them.

Had his feelings for her mom intensified?

It would be just fine with Mia if they had. She wasn't about to stand in the way of her mom's happiness. Especially if that happiness was Travis.

She nudged him gently with her elbow. "Hey, so have you decided to run for town council?"

He didn't answer right away, then finally looked at her and said, "I'll tell you after tomorrow's meeting."

She understood. He wanted to see if it would still be necessary. If Lavinia dropped the injunction and the town council voted for the allowance so that the inn could keep its third story, there would be no pressing reason for Travis to run. Although, part of Mia really wanted to see Lavinia knocked completely off her throne.

Maybe that was petty, but the woman deserved it.

"You'd better get moving," Georgia said. "That sunset isn't going to wait. Don't worry about all this. I'll clean up."

Gulf Coast Secrets

"I'll help you," Griffin said. "Then I'm going to give Chloe a bath."

"I'll help, too." Travis picked up his plate and headed for the sink. "After all, I made most of this mess."

"Nope, I've got it," Georgia said. "Griffin, go use the tub in my bathroom and give Chloe a bath in there. Mia, get those pictures already. When you get back, you can give Clyde his dinner."

"Okay, will do." Mia got up from her seat.

"And Travis, go relax. You did enough work already."

"Yes, ma'am," he said.

"So bossy," Mia said, smiling. It was nice to see her mom being herself again. Mia knew that didn't mean she'd stopped stressing over the council meeting, just that she was handling it better.

They all went to do their things, but Mia was quick about hers. The sun was setting fast and it wasn't hard to get a great picture. She didn't even leave the back deck.

When she went back into the house, she put her phone in her pocket and found Clyde waiting for her by the sofa. "Hungry?"

He meowed. He seemed to know when dinnertime was.

"Come on, you handsome thing. Let's get you some food."

Her mom was still in the kitchen cleaning up. Travis, who'd been told to relax, was actually washing out the big pot he'd used to make the pasta in.

Mia dumped a can of cat food into a bowl for Clyde and set it down on his mat. He went to work on it immediately. She chucked the can in the trash, then got a rag to wipe off the kitchen table with.

Maggie Miller

"Thanks, honey," her mom said.

"Sure. Hey, what are you going to wear tomorrow? For the council meeting? Are you going to dress up? I think you should."

Georgia stopped in the middle of the kitchen. "I hadn't even thought about it." She shook her head. "I don't know if I have anything appropriate. My wardrobe is pretty thin these days."

"You must have something."

Georgia made a face. "Honey, I think you're seriously overestimating what's in my closet."

Mia looked at Travis. "What are you wearing?"

"Khakis with a button-down shirt and a sport coat. That's about as dressed up as I get. Although I might have a tie somewhere if you think I need it."

"No," Mia said. "That sounds fine." Then she looked at her mom again. "Do you have a dress? Nice pants with a blouse?"

Georgia groaned. "I have a sequin cocktail dress that I couldn't bear to part with since I finally fit into it again. The only other thing that might work is a navy pantsuit."

"That sounds extremely uninspiring."

Georgia frowned. "If you want inspiring clothes, you're looking at the wrong woman. I don't have anything that fits that bill."

Mia finished cleaning the table and straightened, smiling. "Actually, you have just the thing."

"I do?"

Mia nodded. "Well, Aunt Norma does."

Gulf Coast Secrets

"You want me to wear something of hers?" Georgia tipped her head. "We are about the same size, now. But what?"

"Are you done cleaning?" Mia asked. "Let's run over to the inn and I'll show you."

Travis nodded. "Go. I can finish. There's not much left to do anyway."

Ten minutes later, they were standing in front of Aunt Norma's closet. Mia pulled the doors open wide and went straight for the suit that seemed like the most logical thing for her mother to wear. "This. This is what you should wear."

"Aunt Norma's Chanel suit?"

Mia nodded. "Travis told us that according to her stories it's what she wore to the council meeting where her allowance was granted. Seems like the perfect thing to wear to the council meeting where the new allowance will be granted."

Georgia shook her head and looked very unconvinced. "I don't know. You said that suit was worth a lot of money."

"It is, but that's no reason *not* to wear it. It certainly didn't stop Aunt Norma and it shouldn't stop you." Mia laid it on the bed. "Besides, it'll be like taking Aunt Norma with us into battle."

Georgia snorted softly. "Okay, you've talked me into it. Maybe. If the suit fits. And I don't look ridiculous."

"Mom, it's Chanel. Just try it on. I want to go look at that secret panel in her office anyway." Mia walked out, leaving her mother to change. She'd had a feeling her mom would be reluctant to wear the suit, but Mia also had a feeling that once Georgia saw herself in the suit, she'd change her mind.

Maggie Miller

Mia's hope was that the suit would give her mom confidence and be a constant reminder of what Norma had done. It really would be like taking her to the council meeting with them.

She opened the door to her aunt's hidden office under the stairs and flipped on the light to inspect the panel in the ceiling. How had she not noticed that? She touched the lock.

"Mia? What do you think?"

She turned around. And smiled broadly at her mom. "You look…amazing. Even better? You look unstoppable."

Gulf Coast Secrets

Chapter Twenty-seven

Georgia had butterflies the size of buzzards in her stomach as they walked into city hall and headed for the community room where the town council meeting was about ten minutes away from taking place. The last time she'd felt like this had been when she'd met with the attorneys about her divorce.

It was nerve-wracking and a little nauseating.

She blew out a long, slow breath, praying her stomach and nerves would both calm down. She put her hand on her belly. Her fingers brushed one of the fancy buttons decorating her borrowed suit.

She smiled. And then she remembered that Norma had been through this already and come out a winner. That helped. A little.

But Norma hadn't been facing the possible destruction of her dream. She'd only been hoping to expand it with that third floor.

Mia slipped her hand into Georgia's as they walked into the community room. "We've got this."

Maggie Miller

Georgia smiled despite her nerves. "I hope so."

Mia leaned in. "Look around you. Look how many people are here to support you."

Georgia took a better look at the room. It was arranged like a small auditorium, its ivory walls unmarked except for the town seal on the wall behind the dais. Industrial blue carpet matched the seats of the folding chairs that had been set up in rows with a center aisle. At the end of that aisle was the dais, a microphone at each seat. Name plates in front of each seat also identified each councilmember.

Lavinia wasn't in hers yet. Georgia tried not to focus on that and what it might mean. She was probably just talking to people.

Sitting near the front was Agatha, Hilda, Mary Lou, and Ellen. They saw her and waved.

She waved back. It was good to see friendly faces.

Another one was approaching them. Mr. Gillum. He had his briefcase with him and looked very official. "Good evening, Ms. Carpenter."

"Hi, Mr. Gillum. Thank you for coming." It helped knowing such a smart, capable man was on her side. It also helped that he'd be presenting her case.

He nodded. "I've been preparing for this all day, and I assure you, our case is as solid as can be. If you'll excuse me, I have to step outside to take a phone call, but I'll come find you when I get back."

"Okay, sounds good." As he left, she looked around a little more.

Griffin, with Chloe on his shoulder and his camera around his neck, had found Kelly and the two were caught up in

Gulf Coast Secrets

animated conversation. As Georgia turned back toward Mia and Travis, a handsome young man came toward them.

"Hey, Mia."

She turned. "Lucas. I didn't know you were going to be here."

He shrugged, smiling a little shyly. "Moral support and all that."

Mia looked at Georgia. "Mom, this is Lucas Ludlow. The store manager."

He held out his hand. "Nice to meet you, Ms. Carpenter."

She shook it. "You, too, Lucas. It was very nice of you to come." No wonder Mia enjoyed her job so much. Lucas was very attractive, and from a mother's perspective, seemed like a real catch.

Although Georgia wasn't sure Mia was ready to dive into another relationship just yet. Georgia knew from personal experience that it took time to get over being betrayed by the person you were supposed to spend the rest of your life with.

The heart had to heal and learn to trust again.

"There are some seats together in the third row." Travis pointed.

"Perfect. Let's take them." She put her hand on Mia's arm. "We're going to sit. Join us when you're ready."

"Okay."

Georgia and Travis made their way through the small crowd to the empty seats. She moved in a few and sat. He went past her and took the next chair.

She glanced around. "Are there always this many people at a town council meeting?"

"Depends on what's on the docket. Tonight seems to be a real barnburner." He snorted. "People are probably hoping for a knockdown, drag out brawl."

"What?"

"Verbally, I mean." He shook his head, smiling. Then he looked at her. "You look great, by the way. Like a woman who's got it all together."

"Do I?" She almost laughed. "That's the suit. Because trust me, I do not feel like that inside."

"Doesn't matter. No one can tell."

"I hope you're right."

He looked past her. "Hey, there's Diego."

"The painter?" She turned to look. "What is he doing here?"

"Well, if you don't get your new allowance he's out of a big job. He's here to support you."

A warm feeling flowed through Georgia. The realization that she had this much support was truly uplifting.

Travis tipped his head. "And there's Alan Crenshaw and his wife, too."

Georgia didn't need to ask why he was here. Alan owned the hardware store, a place that would continue to see income from the inn's rehabilitation efforts if tonight went well. She took a breath. "This is amazing."

"What is?" Travis asked.

"That all these people showed up."

"Not really. They want you to win."

"Or do they want Lavinia to lose?"

He laughed. "Same difference. But yes, I'm sure some of them are here hoping Lavinia gets a little bit of her own

Gulf Coast Secrets

medicine this evening." His eyes narrowed. "I wonder where she is, by the way."

Georgia looked at the dais where the council members were filing in. There was a woman with them, but it wasn't Lavinia. "Maybe she's going to make a grand entrance."

"Could be. You never know with that one."

Roger Gillum joined them with an older woman following along. "Ms. Carpenter, Mr. Taylor, this is Flora Whitman, my administrative assistant."

Travis stood. "Nice to meet you, Ms. Whitman."

She smiled and nodded. "Nice to meet you too. Call me Flora."

Georgia shook her hand. "Call me Georgia then. And thank you for never sounding like you've had enough of me. I feel like I call you all the time and it's always because something in my world is on fire."

Flora laughed. "You get pretty used to that when you work for an attorney, so don't you worry about it. You call whenever you need."

Roger pointed to the row behind Georgia. "We'll sit behind you so your family can have these seats. But I'll still be close enough if you have any questions."

"All right," Georgia said.

They moved back to that row as Griffin, Kelly, Mia, and Lucas arrived. Mia sat next to Georgia with Lucas beside her. Then Kelly, then Griffin at the very end of the row.

Chloe was sleeping in his arm, but if she woke up and started fussing, he needed to be able to get up and out quickly. With his free hand, he lifted his camera and snapped a few shots of the council members on the dais.

Maggie Miller

Georgia wondered if it was possible for her granddaughter to stay asleep throughout the entire meeting. She didn't want Griffin to have to leave, but it was better that he was here at all instead of home, wondering what was going on. Of course, he had to be here. He was supposed to take pictures of the meeting for the paper. If Chloe fussed, maybe Mia could take her so that Griffin could stay and do his job.

The councilman at the center, whose nameplate read Francisco, tapped the gavel. "Please come to order. The council meeting is about to begin."

Lavinia still wasn't present.

Georgia leaned toward Travis and whispered, "Why isn't she here yet?"

He shook his head. "Your guess is as good as mine. But they have a quorum, so it doesn't matter."

Georgia decided that was a good thing so despite her still quavering nerves, she allowed herself to hope a little more.

They stood for the pledge of allegiance, then sat again, listening as the council went through all of its standard procedures. Everyone was thanked for coming. Roll call was next, which made it all the more obvious that Lavinia hadn't shown.

Following that they voted to approve the agenda, which was followed by a report from one of the councilwomen on the state of the town's two parks. Apparently, they'd just gotten new benches and new recycling bins.

It was incredibly dry, boring stuff, but Georgia hung onto every word so that she didn't miss when the conversation shifted to her.

Gulf Coast Secrets

Time dragged on while more reports were read, old business was dealt with, and a motion was made to approve past council meeting minutes.

Georgia glanced at her granddaughter, who was still fast asleep. Not hard to see why. Georgia could have drifted off herself.

Finally, new business was announced. And just like that, Georgia's nerves came rushing back. She knew Mr. Gillum was going to handle the bulk of it, but she also knew there was a good chance she'd be called upon.

Behind her, Roger got to his feet and went to stand in line at the small podium and microphone set up for the audience. He waited his turn behind a woman who was advocating for public hummingbird feeders.

She grabbed Travis's hand. And then Mia's. There was no thought to the movement, other than she needed something to hold on to. Someone, really. And they were sitting beside her.

She kept her eyes on Roger as he approached the microphone. "Good evening, members of the council. I'm Attorney Roger Gillum and I'm here representing Georgia Carpenter in the matter of the town of Blackbird Beach versus the Sea Glass Inn."

The council secretary kept busily typing away at her machine as she took notes.

One of the councilmen leaned toward his microphone. "Your client is required to be present."

"She is." Roger turned toward her.

That was her sign. She stood up, letting go of Mia and Travis's hands. "I'm Georgia Carpenter."

The councilman gave her a nod, then looked at Roger. "Proceed."

"Ms. Carpenter is a new citizen of Blackbird Beach as well as the proprietor of the inn, having recently inherited it from her great aunt, Norma Merriweather, a well-known and much-loved citizen of this town."

A few affirmative murmurs went up from the crowd. That earned them a few stern looks from some of the council members, but nothing was said.

Roger went on. "Two days ago my client was issued an injunction by this council, demanding that all renovation and rehabilitation work on the Sea Glass Inn be stopped immediately. The reason for this as stated in the injunction was that the special allowance made for the inn's third floor only applied to Norma Merriweather's ownership of the inn and did not convey to anyone who had purchased or inherited the inn such as my client Norma Merriweather's great niece, Georgia Carpenter."

A few gasps and a couple of clucked tongues followed that. Along with another slightly less stern look from one of the councilmen.

Georgia took that as an indication that he knew what a mean and petty thing that injunction was. Jack Hannigan, Ellen's boyfriend, looked downright peeved. Georgia hoped that meant Ellen's roast chicken dinner had worked its magic and he was on their side.

Roger had yet to glance at the folder he'd put on the podium. "I ask that you not only rescind that injunction, but also that the council would grant a new allowance for the inn's third floor. I would respectfully request that said allowance would be in perpetuity for the life of the inn regardless of who owns it."

A few of the council members looked like this was the first time they'd heard about this. Could that be true? Or had they just not paid attention to what Lavinia was up to? Did she have that much power?

"There is no downside to granting this new allowance. The Sea Glass Inn provides a great benefit to this town. Not only does it bring visitors to our beautiful town, but those visitors shop at our stores, eat at our restaurants, and spend their money in other places in our town. The increase in revenues benefits all of us. There is no logical reason to prevent Georgia Carpenter from going forward with her plans to reopen the inn."

"I object," Francisco stated. "There is a downside. If we grant one special allowance what's to stop a whole slew of other hotels and motels from seeking the same allowance. We've worked hard to keep this town unspoiled by high rise buildings and cookie cutter condos. You're asking us to throw all of that out of the window."

"No, I'm not," Roger answered. "I'm asking you to grant something that this council had already approved once upon a time. I'm not asking you to change the zoning laws. If it helps, think of this as a transfer of the allowance from one owner to another. Nothing new is being done."

But Francisco didn't seem ready to back down just yet. "Then what do we tell the next land developer or corporation that comes along and wants to put condos on the beach? We could be sued."

Maggie Miller

Roger planted his hands on the podium. "I imagine it would be business as usual and you would refer them to the zoning laws that prohibit such buildings. And if anyone attempts to sue the town because of that, I'll personally take on the case."

That got a little reaction from the crowd. Some laughs and a light smattering of applause.

Roger kept going, possibly to keep Francisco from saying anything else. "Furthermore, it is my professional assessment that the injunction against the Sea Glass Inn is not only punitive but a great detriment to the town as a whole. The tourism industry is something Blackbird Beach has long resisted. Norma Merriweather changed that, and for the better, I might add. Her inn was a beautiful example of hospitality done right. It added to the stellar reputation of our town. Georgia Carpenter looks to continue that legacy."

He took a long look at the seated council members. "Are there any additional questions concerning this matter that I or my client might answer?"

The council members looked at each other, but no one spoke right away. Finally, Francisco leaned into his microphone. "We'll take this matter under advisement and have a decision for you next week."

Roger shook his head. "Respectfully, that's unacceptable. Every day this injunction remains in place it costs my client time and money. We request your decision now. That is well within the bylaws of this meeting. If there is something that remains unclear, please ask and I'll be happy to explain it further. Otherwise, I will be forced to proceed with a countersuit for lost income and personal harassment."

Gulf Coast Secrets

Francisco frowned. "Personal harassment? Now wait just a minute. No one here is harassing your client."

"That's correct." Roger paused. "Because Lavinia Major couldn't be bothered to show up."

Maggie Miller

Gulf Coast Secrets

Chapter Twenty-eight

The feel of Georgia's hand in his had almost caused Travis to lose focus. He knew she'd taken his hand for support and comfort, nothing else. But that hadn't stopped him from enjoying the moment.

The lingering enjoyment of that moment faded when Roger Gillum spoke Lavinia's name. For a second, there was absolute silence. Then a collective gasp went up from the crowd, followed by loud whispers and murmuring that filled the space with a buzz of noise impossible to ignore.

"This meeting will come to order." Councilman Francisco banged the gavel.

The sharp crack of wood on wood woke Chloe up. She immediately started crying, adding to the rising chaos.

"Sorry, Mom." Griffin hopped up and walked out with her.

"It's okay," Georgia said.

The crowd grew louder, possibly emboldened by Chloe's volume. Travis didn't blame them. He felt like doing a little hollering himself.

"Order!" Francisco banged the gavel a second time, but it took a third before people started to settle down. He looked at Gillum. "What do you mean by that statement, Mr. Gillum? It sounds very much like an accusation."

"Because it is. It's an undisputed fact that Lavinia Major and Norma Merriweather were not friends. Ms. Major's authoring of this injunction against the Sea Glass Inn at this precise moment when it is actively being refurbished can easily be construed as punitive. In layman's terms, Ms. Major has an ax to grind with my client solely on the basis of Ms. Carpenter being related to Norma Merriweather."

His gaze took on a steely, undeterred quality. "That's grounds for a personal harassment case if ever I saw one. Ladies and gentlemen of the council, I would finally like to state that if the powers of this organization are going to be used to personally attack the citizens of this town, then I may be filing more than one lawsuit. Serious consideration needs to be given to the actions of your *elected* members."

Georgia leaned over. "Did he just threaten all of them?"

"I believe he did," Travis answered. "While also telling them to do something about Lavinia."

Councilman Hannigan spoke up. "Mr. Gillum, I assure you that such behavior is not, nor has it ever been, the purpose of this council. Your suggestion of consideration will be taken under advisement. I move the council votes on this matter now and puts it to bed. Lavinia knew what was on the docket tonight. To me, her decision not to attend the meeting is telling in its own way."

"You betcha," Agatha shouted.

Laughter filtered through and Francisco raised the gavel in warning. It did the trick as he put it down again without using it.

One of the councilwomen leaned toward her microphone. "I second that. Let's vote now."

Travis tipped his head toward Georgia and whispered, "Victoria Leeds. She owns the flower shop. Your aunt was a regular customer."

Georgia nodded. "Good to know."

Was that the slightest hint of a smile he saw? Or was it just her nerves showing? He couldn't tell. He wanted to take her hand again. Just to show his support. But maybe that moment had passed.

Butch McDowell, the councilman who was also the high school football coach, sighed loudly. "I agree. Let's get this over with. All in favor of killing this injunction and granting a permanent allowance for the third floor of the Sea Glass signify by saying aye."

Francisco started to say something, but he was drowned out by a slew of ayes answering McDowell.

McDowell continued. "All opposed, signify by saying nay."

Francisco breathed into his mike. "Nay."

McDowell nodded at the secretary. "The ayes have it, the injunction is tabled, and the allowance is granted." He looked at Georgia. "Ms. Carpenter, you can pick up your paperwork tomorrow after three P.M." Then he smiled. "Welcome to

Blackbird Beach. We look forward to the revenue the reopening of the Sea Glass Inn will bring to town."

A cheer went up from the crowd that no amount of gavel pounding could squelch. Half of the audience was on their feet, including Georgia, Mia, Lucas, and Kelly. All of the bridge club ladies were up, too. Griffin had come back in and was snapping pictures one-handed with Chloe on his shoulder. Georgia was hugging Mia.

Travis raised his fist and let out a whoop.

Then Georgia was hugging him. "Roger did it!"

Travis hugged her back, marveling at how good she smelled. "He sure did."

The thump, thump, thump of the gavel finally settled the crowd down again, along with a little lecture from Francisco. "Enough. If you cannot be quiet and hold your comments, you will be asked to leave. This meeting has *not* been adjourned."

Everyone sat down.

"Now, is there any new business?"

There was, unfortunately. A proposal to install a streetlight at the corner of Perkins and Dale. A complaint about the noise from the garbage trucks coming by too early in the morning. An appeal for a ten p.m. curfew for all residents under the age of eighteen during the school months.

That was met with a few snickers, a loud snort, and one reluctant round of clapping.

As the new business droned on, Travis looked at Georgia. She was grinning from ear to ear, and he couldn't blame her. He felt the same way. They'd won. Decisively.

Gulf Coast Secrets

She looked back at him, her smile somehow widening. "I'm happy," she whispered.

He nodded. "Me, too."

She slipped her hand into his again, surprising him. "Thank you."

He wasn't sure what she was thanking him for, but he'd take it. He smiled and sat back.

The rest of the meeting seemed to fly by after that. But when it was finally adjourned, the quick exit he'd expected them to make didn't happen.

Georgia, it seemed, had become a bit of a celebrity.

Not only did the ladies from the bridge club gather around, but so did a lot of other folks eager to make her acquaintance and welcome her to town. There were a lot of mentions of Norma, how much she was missed, how much she'd done for the town, what a wonderful person she was.

All things that made him smile. And all good things for Georgia to hear.

He stood back and let her have her moment, taking pleasure in how gracious she was with people. He was reminded again of Norma and her way of making everyone seem like they were the center of her attention, even if that attention only lasted thirty seconds.

Whatever that skill was, Georgia had it.

He smiled. The inn was going to be as successful as ever. Maybe more so.

Diego came up to him. "We good for me to start tomorrow?"

Maggie Miller

"Absolutely. I was going to call you. After this meeting, no one can challenge the injunction and we'll have the new allowance by the afternoon, so let's get started."

"I'll be there with my crew at eight." He clapped Travis on the shoulder. "Congrats, man. Gotta say, that was fun to watch."

Travis chuckled. "Yeah, it was. See you in the morning."

Roger Gillum joined him next. "I don't want to interrupt Georgia, but will you let her know that if the paperwork isn't ready tomorrow on time to call me? I'll be happy to get after them if it's a minute late."

"I will. Thank you for helping her with this. She couldn't have done it without you."

He smiled. "I think Norma would be pleased, don't you?"

"I think she'd be pouring shots of bourbon right now."

Roger laughed. "That she would. Good night, Mr. Taylor."

"Good night, Mr. Gillum."

Travis stood watching Georgia for a few more minutes. Griffin was nearby and still snapping away one-handed, but then Chloe started to fuss and that was that. Griffin tried to settle her, but she wasn't having it. He started out the door with her.

"We have to go," Georgia announced. "My granddaughter has had enough. It was so nice to meet all of you. I hope to see you all again very soon."

With Mia at her side, she joined Travis. "Let's go. I'm a little exhausted."

"I bet."

Gulf Coast Secrets

They went straight out to the sidewalk. Griffin was fastening Chloe into her car seat. He looked up. "I have to take her home."

"I know. You want help?" Georgia asked.

He shook his head, smiling. "Go celebrate."

She nodded. "Okay, see you at the house."

"Yep." He gave a quick smile to Kelly. She smiled back. Then he got behind the wheel and drove off.

"I need to go, too," Kelly said. "I want to write up my notes about this meeting while they're still fresh. This is a pretty big story for the paper. I want to do it right."

"I appreciate that," Georgia said. "Thank you for all your help."

"You're welcome. Have a good night." She gave them a wave and walked away toward her car.

"We should celebrate," Mia said.

Lucas, still standing with them, nodded. He pointed across the street to the Fork and Spoon diner. "We could go have ice cream sundaes."

"That sounds perfect," Mia said. "I'm in."

She and Lucas headed for the curb so they could cross.

Travis turned to Georgia. "What do you think? Are you in the mood for a banana split?"

"I'm more of a hot fudge girl myself." Then she looked down at her suit. "I just can't afford to spill."

He laughed. "I have a feeling you'll be able to afford all sorts of things soon." He offered her his arm. "Come on, let's go indulge."

Maggie Miller

She took it and they started across the street after Mia and Lucas. A waitress seated them all in a booth, him and Georgia on one side. Lucas and Mia on the other.

It felt like a double date. But maybe that was just wishful thinking on his part.

Georgia was true to her word and ordered a hot fudge sundae. He went with the tin roof, while Mia got a salted caramel and Lucas had a banana split.

Georgia spooned up a big serving of vanilla ice cream dripping in hot fudge. "I can already tell this is going to be amazing."

The moment the spoon was in her mouth, she started nodding. "Mmm-hmm. Amazing."

He laughed. "This was the right way to celebrate."

"For sure," Mia said. "I can't remember the last time I had ice cream."

"Me, too." Lucas smiled. He seemed to be content to just be near her.

Georgia finished her mouthful. "I don't know about you guys, but I'm beat. Like I've been wrung out. Not physically, but mentally and emotionally. And to think Lavinia didn't even show up."

Travis nodded. "I think that was her way of doing the right thing without actually having to do it. The right thing by default."

"Yeah," Mia said. "By not being there, she didn't have to accept blame for any of it either."

"Except," Lucas said, "I think there will be some fallout. People know what she's done now."

Gulf Coast Secrets

"True." Mia nodded. "Hey, Travis, what's the deal with that Francisco guy? He seemed like he was on Lavinia's side."

"He did," Travis agreed. "He's an accountant. That's about all I know about him. Maybe he does her books. Or maybe he and Lavinia are a thing? He's a little young for her, though."

Georgia shook her head. "I don't want to think about that."

Mia gestured with her spoon. "I guess Kelly won't publish those pictures now. We should have asked her."

Georgia shook her head. "I'm sure she won't. But the fact that she has them...that ought to be a good deterrent for any future nonsense out of Lavinia."

"I'd like to think that's true." Travis shrugged. "But you never really know with that one."

"Well, if she does come back at us somehow, we have insurance." Georgia used her spoon to rescue a dollop of hot fudge headed over the rim of the glass. "She'd have to come clean about her past if those pictures get out. She'd have to admit she lied. And I don't think she's about to do that."

Travis nodded. "I'm not going to worry about her until there's a reason to. We have too much work to do. Now that we can do it."

"Oh!" Georgia looked at him. "Can you call Diego and see when he can get us back on his schedule for painting?"

"Tomorrow morning. Eight a.m."

She smiled. "You're the best."

He laughed. "I really am."

Her smiled turned into something deeper, something he couldn't name so much as he could feel. "I'm excited to get back to work. It should be smooth sailing from here on out. Well, so long as Mr. Gillum can squash my ex's claim that he's due a share of my inheritance."

"Gillum will get it done." Travis certainly hoped so. Georgia had been through enough.

Tonight's win was outstanding, but it wouldn't matter if her soon-to-be-ex husband got his hands in the pie.

Gulf Coast Secrets

Chapter Twenty-nine

The sky was blue, the sun was bright, the air was crisp, and Georgia's entire being was filled with the kind of unstoppable joy that made all the world seem right. Even her coffee tasted better. She smiled as she stared out at the ocean from the back deck.

Today was the first day of getting the inn back on track and she had never been so ready for anything in all her life. She took a deep breath, savoring the salty tang in the air.

"Mom?" Mia stuck her head out. "I'm off to work. Let me know how things go."

"Will do. Have a good day. Love you."

"Love you, too. Later."

Griffin walked out a few moments later, coffee in one hand, Chloe in the other. "It's awfully bright out here."

Georgia laughed. "You want me to take her so you can drink your coffee?"

"No, it's okay. I'm good." He smiled. "I promise you can look after her later today all you want."

He sat in one of the Adirondack chairs. "Kelly texted me this morning. Word on the street is Lavinia's in big trouble. The council may censure her."

"What does that mean?"

He shrugged. "It's basically a slap on the wrist, but it's also a permanent mark against her."

"I guess it's something." But Georgia couldn't find the energy to be all that bothered. She'd gotten what she'd wanted. A free and clear path to reopening the inn.

He fixed the blanket that Chloe was wrapped in. "What's on the To Do list today?"

"More work in the kitchen. Travis finished the painting, but he's going to put in the new light fixture this morning. He might pull up the old linoleum, too, so he can start prepping for the new tile floor."

"I could help with that."

"I'm sure he'd appreciate that. I don't know how easy it'll be getting that linoleum up. Or even if one person can really do it on their own."

"I'm definitely available. Anything else I can take care of?"

She thought a moment. "There's touch up painting that needs to be done in just about every room."

He nodded. "I'm happy to take that on."

"Okay, good. I have to research outdoor furniture today. The entire back deck as well as the front porch needs furnishing. But I'm not ordering it until that allowance paperwork is in my hands."

"You're not worried about that, are you?"

"Not worried. Just…want to be sure." She smiled. "I guess I don't want to jinx it."

Gulf Coast Secrets

He smiled. "I can understand that. Have you heard anything from Dad recently?"

She shook her head. "No. But since Mr. Gillum's working on sorting that whole mess out, I'm taking your father's silence as a good thing. If he thought he was winning, he'd be gloating."

Griffin frowned. "I can't believe dad is being such a jerk. I'm sorry about him, Mom. At least you got us out of the deal."

"Exactly." She smiled as she went over to bend down and kiss her son's head. "You and Mia are all I need, too." She touched Chloe's back. "And sweet pea, too, of course."

"Thanks, Mom." He sighed. "I am so glad to be here."

"I'm so glad you're here too. No rush getting over to the inn this morning either. Make sure you get some breakfast."

"Did you eat?"

She nodded. "I had a yogurt and a banana. But there's cereal or eggs if you feel like cooking."

"Cereal's fine. I still need to shower too."

"You want me to watch Chloe?"

"She'll be all right in her carrier. Won't take me long."

"Okay." Georgia finished her last sip of coffee. "See you over there."

"Yep. See you in a bit."

She walked back into the house, grabbed her purse, made sure she had her phone, then put her coffee mug in the dishwasher and went out the front door.

Two trucks were already parked outside of the Inn. Both were loaded with tools and scaffolding. One had a DS Painters sign on the side of it.

Maggie Miller

Diego got out of that truck as she approached. "Morning, Ms. Carpenter."

She smiled. "Morning, Diego. Call me Georgia, please. Are you guys getting ready to set up?"

"Yep." He looked at the inn as his guys got out of the trucks. "It's not a small job so it won't be fast."

"I don't need it to be fast. I just want it to be good."

He grinned. "After last night? It will be the best job I've ever done."

She laughed. "What does that mean?" He didn't think she'd send Roger after him if she wasn't happy, did he?

He reached into the truck for his travel mug of coffee. "Do you have any idea how many people are going to be visiting? Checking on this place to see how work is going? I could book enough business off this job to fill the rest of my year."

"You really think so?"

He nodded. "You'd better believe it."

"I hope you do get a year's worth of work. And I hope we get a year's worth of guests. Or more."

"I don't think you'll have anything to worry about with that." He looked at his guys getting out of the second truck. "All right let's get moving. Start on the right side."

With a collective nod, they began taking the scaffolding off the trucks.

"Have a good day, Diego." She started toward the inn.

"You too."

She paused. "Hey, have you seen Travis?"

He nodded. "He just went back inside to get me a key to the shed so we can store our equipment in it and lock it up overnight."

Gulf Coast Secrets

"Okay, thanks." She walked down the path to the front porch, went up the steps and found the door unlocked, as she'd expected. "Travis? I'm here."

He stuck his head around the corner from Norma's office. "Hey. Just trying to find a key for Diego. Do you know where the shed key is?"

"It should be hanging—"

"Never mind, found it." He came walking out. "It was hanging on the hook on the corkboard. Where it was supposed to be."

She grinned.

He shook his head. "I need more coffee."

"Then go get a cup after you give him the key."

"I will. Back in a bit." He hesitated, smiling. "Good morning, by the way."

"Good morning."

His smile got a little bigger as he went by.

So did hers as she walked back to the kitchen. The pale yellow paint had dried beautifully, leaving the walls a gorgeous soft, buttery color. Just being in the space made her happy. She thought Norma would have approved, especially after she'd painted her bedroom a similar color.

But being in the kitchen also reminded Georgia that she still had staff to hire. A cook and a couple of housekeepers at least. Of course, that all hinged on there being guests. But Diego seemed to think that wouldn't be problem.

She was starting to believe that too.

"Mom?"

"In the kitchen, Griff."

He walked in, looking around as he did. "Man, looks great." He had Chloe in her carrier, as well as her diaper bag, another plastic grocery store bag, and his camera bag.

"Thanks."

"I'm going to put Chloe in the crib and set up that mobile that Mia got her, then I'm ready to get to work. Mia wants some shots of the scaffolding going up and the guys getting to work on the exterior."

"Okay. We're just getting started in here ourselves. Travis went to give Diego a key, then he's going to his place for another cup of coffee so we have to wait until he's back to find out where the paint is that you'll need for touching up the rooms."

"All right. I'll work on putting that mobile on the crib then." He held Chloe up in the air, making her laugh. "Let's get you set up, kiddo."

He went to the breakfast room and Georgia walked through the kitchen to the bedroom that would very soon be hers. She and Mia had left the closet open when they'd come to get the suit, which was still hanging up at the cottage.

"We did it, Aunt Norma," she said softly. "Thank you for those photos. They made all the difference. The suit helped too."

A few minutes later, Travis returned. The three of them spent the rest of the day working inside as Diego and his team tackled the exterior.

Mia joined them when her shift at Ludlow's was done, braving the tall step ladder to clean the enormous chandelier in the foyer. "I'm tired of seeing this amazing thing covered in dust."

Gulf Coast Secrets

"Go for it," Georgia said. "Did you get a before picture? Because I think you'll be sorry if you do all that work and don't have a before and after to show just how much you did."

"Oh, good idea." She climbed back down and got her phone out. "Any word on the allowance being ready yet?"

Georgia shook her head. "They said not until three. I don't imagine it'll be sooner than that."

Mia got her pictures, put her phone away, and went back up the ladder with her rags and window spray. "I just thought maybe they'd be early."

The tiniest ripple of nerves went through Georgia. Was there any chance the council would change their minds? They couldn't, though, could they? Not after so many people had heard them announce the allowance would be given. They couldn't go back on something they'd done publicly, could they?

"Hey." Mia gave her mother a stern look. "Don't."

"Don't what?"

"Go there. I can see the wheels turning in your head. They're not going to cancel the allowance. They wouldn't dare. The town would be in an uproar. Not to mention Roger would be all over them. And he'd probably enjoy it."

"I know, you're right, but it's human nature to think about the worst-case scenario. At least my human nature, anyway."

"Well, stop it." She grinned as she began polishing the dangling crystals. "That shade of purple you picked out is really bold."

Georgia frowned. "What shade of purple?"

"For the outside of the building."

Georgia froze. "What? It's not supposed to be purple, it's supposed to be Caribbean Blue."

Mia started laughing, the kind of wicked little giggle she did when she was up to something.

Georgia put her hands on her hips and stared at her prankster child. "Very funny. For your information, Diego told me they have at least two days of prep work before they can even start painting the outside."

"And yet, you fell for it." Mia looked down and winked at her. "Relax, Mom. It's all going to be just fine."

"Get to work," Georgia said with a smile.

"Yes, boss."

Already Georgia could see the difference in the crystals Mia had cleaned. The octopus chandelier was going to be spectacular. What a fun way to welcome guests. "Looks better already."

"Really? Cool. Too bad it's going to take forever."

"Well, keep at it. I'm going outside to see how things are progressing. Back in a bit." As Georgia stepped onto the porch, her phone buzzed.

She took it from her pocket and checked the caller ID. It wasn't a number she recognized but with everything going on at the Inn, she didn't dare miss a call that might be important.

"Hello?"

"Georgia, where on earth are you?"

Georgia blinked, her brain processing the familiar voice but still not registering it. "Lilly?"

"Yes, Lilly. Who else would be calling you?"

Georgia shook her head, shaking off her bewilderment at the same time. She hadn't heard her sister's voice in so long

Gulf Coast Secrets

she was a little surprised she recognized it. "Oh, just about a dozen other people I can think of. Not to mention we haven't talked in at least two years."

"Don't be difficult."

Georgia's mouth opened but she couldn't find a nice way to answer. So she didn't.

"You and Robert are getting a divorce."

It wasn't a question so much as a statement, but Georgia responded anyway. "Yes, I know. But thanks for the reminder. How did you find out?"

But Georgia already knew. Lilly *had* to have spoken to Robert. Why on earth had she done that?

"I'm at your *house*, Georgia."

"My house? You mean the one Robert still lives in?"

"What other house would I mean?"

"Well, that hasn't been my house in almost nine months. I've moved."

Lilly sighed. She'd probably rolled her eyes too. "Yes, I figured that out. Where are you? I need to see you."

"*You* need to see *me*." Georgia put her hand on her head. "Lilly, you've never needed to see me."

"Well, I do now."

Georgia closed her eyes and took a breath. This wasn't going to go well. She already knew that. She rattled off the address anyway. "12 Sea Glass Lane in Blackbird Beach."

There was a pause before Lilly spoke again. "You're at Aunt Norma's? That makes perfect sense. I should have known you'd run there. Well, tell the old bird I'll see you both soon. But if you move again before I get there, send me a text, will you?"

Maggie Miller

Georgia didn't want to tell her the truth about Norma over the phone. "Why are you coming? What's going on? How long before you're here?"

"I'll explain when I get there. Probably in about four hours or so. Now I have to drive." She hung up.

Georgia glared at her phone as if it was responsible for this new problem. She couldn't imagine why Lilly was coming to visit, but there was something else Georgia knew without question.

Her sister would flip when she found out that Norma had left the inn and the two cottages to Georgia. And when Lilly went on a rampage, there was no telling what she might do.

Georgia had only one option. Call a family meeting and explain that a storm was on the way.

Gulf Coast Secrets

Want to know when Maggie's next book comes out? Then don't forget to sign up for her newsletter!

Also, if you enjoyed the book, please recommend it to a friend. Even better yet, leave a review and let others know.

Other Books by Maggie Miller:
Gulf Coast Cottage
Gulf Coast Secrets
Gulf Coast Reunion
Gulf Coast Sunsets
Gulf Coast Moonlight

Maggie Miller

About Maggie:

Maggie Miller thinks time off is time best spent at the beach, probably because the beach is her happy place. The sound of the waves is her favorite background music, and the sand between her toes is the best massage she can think of.

When she's not at the beach, she's writing or reading or cooking for her family. All of that stuff called life.

She hopes her readers enjoy her books and welcomes them to drop her a line and let her know what they think!

Maggie Online:

www.maggiemillerauthor.com
www.facebook.com/MaggieMillerAuthor

Made in the USA
Monee, IL
01 November 2025